I0819985

Security Through Absurdity

BOOK THREE
THE BIG SHOW

Rachael L. McIntosh

EntropyPress

Also available by Rachael L McIntosh

Security Through Absurdity Series:

Book 1: Little Yellow Stickies

Book 2: Bubbles Will Pop

Security Through Absurdity
The Big Show

EntropyPress books may be ordered through booksellers or by contacting:

EntropyPress

www.entropypress.com
EntropyPress
PO Box 2254
East Greenwich, RI 02818
USA

ISBN - 13 : 978-0-692-50445-1

Security Through Absurdity

BOOK THREE

THE BIG SHOW

Rachael L. McIntosh

EntropyPress

"Conspiracy theorists of the world, believers in the hidden hands of the Rothschilds and the Masons and the Illuminati, we skeptics owe you an apology. You were right. The players may be a little different, but your basic premise is correct: The world is a rigged game."

-Matt Taibbi

CHAPTER ONE

North Kingstown, Rhode Island, USA
Autumn

THE ANGLES OF THE TINY yellow house were closing in on Jocelyn as the shadows grew longer and more defined. Sure, she had just busted Ethan for some sort of affair, and he had taken off with the kids about fifteen minutes ago. That was depressing enough, but now a power outage?

"Great," she grumbled as she stared at the lifeless computer screen staring back at her. Jocelyn rubbed her temples and then hoisted herself out of the chair. She pushed open the Home Depot French doors that Ethan had installed and cut through the Martha Stewart color palette of the living room with its hardly ever used fireplace and random sampling of the kids' toys.

As she walked into the kitchen, she pulled her long strawberry blond hair back into a loose ponytail and zeroed in on the refrigerator. She had to check. Yup, it wasn't working either. She slowly closed the stainless steel door and tried to remember what the deal was with the circuit breakers. She knew they were in the basement, so she reached behind the fridge, got the key, and unlocked the basement door. They kept the door locked because there were guns down there.

Jocelyn had insisted when they moved into the place, right before the twins were born, that the kids never have access to Ethan's guns. Ever. This request (well, it was more like a demand) had taken Ethan by surprise. Ethan Lowe was a former Navy Seal, and guns were a big part of his lifestyle growing up. Of course, they had both worked for the Conglomerate, a huge private defense contracting operation.

He had worked for the mercenary division, and she, Ms. Jocelyn McLaren, had been in the marketing department while he had been rolling around in Iraq. Mr. and Ms. America, really.

But that was five years ago, back when Ethan still loved her, and they were both all excited to have left their jobs and started a new life. They had made plans, and it was going to be a great little family. But things changed. Now Ethan was barely ever around, she was bankrupt, they had two little mouths to feed, and she felt like she spent most of her time doing laundry.

Jocelyn fiddled with the basement key. She didn't like going down those basement stairs. Not only were they something of a physical challenge because of the multiple sclerosis she was managing, but the basement steps were downright creepy. She had a really bad dream about these stairs once, and since then she rarely went down into the basement. She braced herself and ended up lumbering down the dank stairway while en route to randomly flip circuit breaker switches. Finally, she decided to just call the power company and report an outage. She concluded that someone must have crashed into a telephone pole or something.

While searching for her cell phone, a terrible thought struck her: maybe the person who crashed into the pole and left her in the dark was Ethan. Maybe he had been so upset and distracted by their earlier confrontation... *I really hope he and the kids are okay.*

She headed out to the front yard with her cell phone because, of course, the reception inside the house wasn't that great. She got through to the power company, and after dealing with the phone tree and waiting on hold for way too long, she was informed that no lines were down. According to them, everything was functioning perfectly.

But things weren't perfect. She thought about it, cringed and decided to call Ethan. It was his house after all. He had done the re-wiring during the renovations. Maybe she was doing something wrong. Maybe it was an easy fix.

As soon as he answered, Jocelyn knew something wasn't right. He was way too calm. Uncharacteristically calm. He didn't even sound like himself and she wasn't prepared for what he was telling her.

"You mean *you* shut off the electricity *and* the phone?"

"Yup," Ethan answered casually.

"But... I'm here. I'm still here," she blurted into the cell phone.

"I know. That's why I shut it all off."

"Huh? But why?"

"Because I'm taking the kids to New Hampshire. To go camping... I think. Hey, kids! You wanna go on your first real camping trip? I'll show you how the gun works!" Her heart sunk to her stomach at the thought of him with a gun and the kids. She heard an overwhelming shout of approval from the peanut gallery and Ethan continued, "I'll be back with them soon. Don't worry. They'll have a good time." Jocelyn was at a loss for words as he kept talking. "But I'm not leaving *you* there with the Internet and electric that *I* pay for. I'm not paying for you to sit in front of a computer, Jocelyn. And I don't need to be paying for the phone. You've got a cell phone."

The sun was starting to set. Bright slashes of the dwindling daylight sliced through the trees. Jocelyn couldn't believe this. She wandered over to the driveway to get better reception. She stood right where his truck had been when she last saw him loading the kids into it, and that's when she noticed the dangling cables on the corner of the house. *He cut the wires to his own house?! When did he...?*

Jocelyn spoke cautiously, "Ethan. The wires to the house... The wires aren't connected anymore."

"Joss, you're breaking up. The juice boxes are in the red cooler, Lilly," she heard him shouting to her daughter.

A swelling wave of anxiety rushed through Jocelyn's body, and she almost dropped her phone; the same cell phone

Ethan's misguided text message to someone called Heartbreaker had showed up on earlier that day and prompted her to tell him to leave. She could hear her twins, Lillian and William, babbling in the background. Still holding the phone to her ear, she ran back into the house to get her car keys and asked, "Where are you now?" Maybe she could cut him off somewhere and wrangle the kids back.

"What?"

"Where are you now?!" she shouted into the phone.

"In the Super Stop and Shop parking lot. We just loaded up."

"So, you're leaving this minute? It's pretty late to be leaving on a road trip with five-year-olds, don't you think?"

"Nah. They'll be fine. I've packed a cooler with everything they could ever want. We'll sleep in the truck and be home in about a week." He said like it was no big deal.

"Oh, okay, so you're all suddenly going camping, and I'm staying here alone in the dark?" She was completely confused by what was going on. Sure, their relationship had gotten strange for her a while ago, but he had never done anything as whacked out as this before. Jocelyn was trying to stay calm. She didn't want to ignite any sort of internal fuse in him because he had the kids and was armed, and he certainly wasn't thinking like a normal person.

"*You* told me to take the kids somewhere—that *you* needed time. Well, that's what I'm doing. I'm helping *you* out here, Joss," he said over the sound of his truck starting up. "I can't pay for all this. I mean, I came back in the house to get the Glock, and you didn't even hear me. You were so involved in whatever it was you were doing on the computer."

"You did?" Jocelyn thought back to what she was doing before the lights went out and realized that she had, in fact, been completely engrossed in finding out the current price of gold. "Well, it's not like you let me know you were back."

"Well," he said, mocking her tone, "it's not like you

would have cared. You only seem to care about that Ray Pierce campaign and his cult and..."

She cut him off as she swung open the car door and hopped inside. "It's not Ray Pierce! It's a book club, and I don't think..."

"Whatever. I'm not paying for it. You can go to your mother's and let her finance your apathy." He hung up. Jocelyn threw the phone onto the passenger seat and tore out toward Super Stop and Shop.

CHAPTER TWO

TEMPORARILY TUCKED INTO A CHEAP Howard Johnson's off Route 95 in Warwick, Rhode Island, Mišel Gujic wondered how the place was even able to stay in business. It literally smelled like shit. The motel was positioned across the highway from a sewage treatment plant, and the residual scent of processed fecal matter, if left unchecked, could leave evidence of her trail. She had never been busted after twenty-two successful hit jobs... Well, one wasn't a complete success—the pregnant lady. She'd killed off the wrong woman and didn't get paid.

Regardless of that little snafu, Mišel, although lower on the list of preferred contractors, still had a decent reputation. She was slippery and sneaky and never got caught. Her specialty: poison. Her excellent verbal and written American English, along with being a pretty good typist, allowed her entry as a temporary worker when the job called for it. A whole slate of seemingly legit aliases were at her disposal. Her real name, Mišel Gujic, was never used, of course. She had passports and driver's licenses with names like: Mishel Smith, Michelle Anderson, and Shelly Johnson.

Her looks didn't hurt, either. She was completely non-descript with mousey features that were easily obscured by a new hairstyle or different frames. In fact, the only thing witnesses were ever able to agree on was that she wore glasses. Every so often, people even mistook her for a man with her short haircut.

The thing that made this woman-of-many-names valuable was that no one could ever prove that the person she had just killed had been poisoned. She was an expert chemist and knew how to concoct specialty blends designed specifically for her victims that eluded standard toxicology reports.

She hoisted the red reversible JANSPORT duffle bag over her shoulder and headed to the lobby.

"Did you enjoy your stay with us, Miss Jones? I hope everything was to your liking," the front desk attendant asked as he hurriedly stashed away the Wizard air freshener canister before accepting her returned key and small stack of twenties. The man seemed to be bracing himself for the standard complaint and was clearly surprised that she didn't even mention it. Mišel just adjusted her horn rims, smiled and headed out the front door, knowing full well that the smell of sewage would be even more pronounced once outside.

She walked purposefully through the parking lot and out to the main road where she hailed a cab.

"Where to?"

"Mind taking me to a laundromat?" she asked while drawing attention to the red bag slung over her shoulder. "Maybe one closer to the airport?"

"Sure, hop in."

On the way to the laundromat, Mišel looked at the plane tickets. Tampa. She was going to Florida to meet up with Heartbreaker. But first the smell. She had to get rid of this damn smell.

CHAPTER THREE

Basel, Switzerland

TIMOTHY BRUCKER ADJUSTED HIS GOLD cuff links while waiting for the response. Although he looked presentable in his Ermenegildo Zegna, it paled in comparison to the suit Jonas Ledergerber had on, a dark charcoal gray Brioni, carefully stitched together with threads of fine white gold. Tim wasn't exactly sure when he became aware of the particulars of men's luxury suits. It had happened almost organically as he adapted to his surroundings over the past thirty years. Only a decade ago, Tim would have been incredibly impressed with Ledergerber and his suit. However, both only served to irritate him now—that, and if he didn't get some nicotine in him within the next four minutes, he was going to lose his mind.

"Mr. Brucker, are you attempting to blackmail me?" Ledergerber asked with a hint of mild amusement as he stood with his back to Brucker, looking out the floor to ceiling windows toward the Art Basel building. "You realize, of course, that media stories about corruption are irrelevant. You are dealing with an untouchable matrix organization." He turned, studied Tim, and strode casually toward his enormous modern art inspired desk. "My dear man," he sighed as he made himself comfortable in his executive chair positioned in front of an eight-foot-tall, original Jackson Pollock oil painting. "I have no idea how you got here, but perhaps I should let you in on a little secret, no?"

"And what would that be?" Tim asked and crossed his arms across his chest. This visit wasn't going the way he had expected. He had hoped that Ledergerber would flinch when he mentioned the Conglomerate, the congressman, and the shenanigans at the tiny division in eastern Connecticut. But it was becoming disastrously apparent that Tim was out of his league as he glanced over at his cell phone on the end table next to him. A text message had just popped up and caught his eye.

GOLD :US $1759.14
OIL: $99.40
NYSE: GLOM $70.58
DJIA: 12983

The little digital flash reminded Tim that Jocelyn McLaren was probably still in danger. She was a loose thread dangling from the Conglomerate's tightly knit web, and someone was going to snip it. She wouldn't be the first one to lose her life, and it wasn't her fault that she was mixed up in any of it anyway. It was just that her former manager, Robert King, was probably going to run for office or be appointed to some lofty position integral to the continued success of the Conglomerate, and naturally, it was important that she be somehow silenced. Paid off is what he would have preferred, and that's how she ended up with the butterfly brooch. Unfortunately for him, and even more unfortunately for Jocelyn, no one had really explained to her what that pin was all about.

He had recently even flown up to Rhode Island because of this situation and discovered that the frustrated assassin he had met with at the International House of Pancakes was taking orders from a bigger fish in the food chain and wasn't changing course. Following this chain of command, Tim was surprised that he ended up here, in Basel, Switzerland.

It was funny how that worked. If he backtracked the trail of people with prices on their heads, a whole world of opportunity opened up for him. It wasn't so much that Tim cared if Jocelyn lived or died. It was the people who wanted her dead who interested him. The people who had folks wiped off the map had money—money enough to pay for just about anything. Those same people usually had secrets that they needed kept secret if they planned to interface with "normal people." However, it was becoming clear that Ledergerber did not deal with, nor was he much concerned about, the average person. Tim was slowly appreciating that Ledergerber was more like a doorman, or a concierge, or something, standing guard at the entrance of a dimension he had little to no knowledge of. He *really* needed some nicotine as this realization hit home.

Ledergerber cracked a silhouette of a smile. "At the end of World War II, the United States put its intelligence agencies in the financing business. Non-transparent people in power, with a license to kill, operating under the cover of government authority, were given the task of growing a hidden funding source for their covert operations. This was accomplished via typical organized crime scenarios—narcotics trafficking, the slave trade, extortion. The money continued to grow unbridled as there were, of course, no taxes to pay or regulations to follow." He smoothed what Tim had identified as a grotesquely expensive Christian Lacroix necktie and continued. "These successful black-market businesses soon partnered with the very enemies the U.S. had been fighting during the war. The Nazis and the Japanese became integral to this U.S. dominated syndicate."

"Well, that's an interesting history lesson," Tim remarked. "I'm a little more concerned about the here and now." He was getting a fingernail-scratching-on-chalkboard headache. He needed nicotine, and this guy droning on wasn't helping.

"Well, you did not let me finish, did you?" Ledergerber smiled like a cat playing with a mouse. "This shadow banking sector in the U.S. is now growing larger than the conventional financial sector. And it will continue to grow. The invisible pillars of this black money will soon hold up the entire U.S.

economy and, by default, the world. So, I am afraid that your claims of me somehow being involved with what you call 'criminal activity' are fairly pointless. Everyone in America is involved in this endeavor when they move money around, which they continue to happily do on a daily basis. By simply making a purchase, Americans contribute to the laundering of blood money. Believe me, Mr. Brucker, the terrorists do not hate you for your freedom."

"You have an interesting perspective, Mr. Ledergerber. I tend to doubt that everyone is as guilty as you and your associates. I have a witness and evidence. We have laws and we have—"

Jonas Ledergerber burst out laughing, and it took Tim by surprise.

"You are not understanding this, my good sir." Ledergerber casually crossed his legs as he regained composure. "Let me draw this out for you before you must depart. The American Dream. Owning a piece of real estate, no? You are familiar with a thing called HUD, are you not?"

"Sure, anyone who has attempted to buy a house knows what HUD is—the Department of Housing and Urban Development. It's a federal government thing, and they give out grants or credits to homebuyers."

"Very good, Mr. Brucker. Now, how would you feel if I told you that the promotion of your 'American Dream' was a money laundering scheme for the dark economy I just described? A criminal enterprise operated by the New York FED, New York FED member banks, the Department of the Treasury, Department of Justice, a handful of intelligence agencies and the military. All this is currently overseen by a prominent defense contractor, Lockheed Martin, for a contract valued at $150,000,000. This movement of money is engineered and approved at the highest levels of your government. The president himself is aware of this activity as HUD is a Cabinet department thanks to Lyndon B. Johnson. We are talking about money on the scale of a leveraged buyout of the entire planet. Bubbles do not pop without presenting significant opportunity, and rest assured, everything happens for a reason. Wealth is ultimately created when people are left dreamless."

Tim watched in silence as Ledergerber plucked a microscopic piece of lint off his sleeve and hastily brushed away any insulting remains before he continued. "You will see an influx of new citizens arriving in your country in an attempt to move this money above ground. The accounts are already set up and the contracts signed. Within your lifetime, this shadow banking system will overtake and effectively blend with outdated economies and currencies. The product of this coupling will become the primary means of exchange, thus ensuring existence for the entire planet. It is my job to make sure this process proceeds seamlessly for the shareholders."

At the mention of the word 'shareholders' Tim reflexively asked, "And who might these shareholders be?"

Ledergerber looked surprised by the question and shook his head as if in pity. "It would be wise to recognize your master, no?"

Not quite knowing how to respond, Tim shifted his weight in the chair and said almost hopefully, "The next presidential election will force debate. There is a candidate who wants to end the Federal Reserve and—"

"Are you not aware that the whole political process in the United States is a controlled exercise? The outcome of which has very little to do with the progression of events?"

Tim sighed, knowing that his negotiations were going absolutely nowhere. "I guess I'd have to be an idiot not to pick up on that at this point."

Mr. Ledergerber reached across his desk and into a little wooden box sitting next to the H.R. Giger cast bronze of what looked like a fetus or tiny baby wearing welding goggles, and produced a cigarette. He lit it with a match and offered one to Tim.

"No. No, thank you. I don't smoke."

"Well, then," Ledergerber huffed, "what good are you to me if I can't even share a cigarette with you?" The double doors of the office opened and what appeared to be a well-dressed executive stood waiting to escort Tim out. "Good day, sir," Ledergerber said casually as he motioned to the door with his cigarette.

Tim stood up, grabbed his cell phone, nodded to Ledergerber and tried not to look too hurried as he exited the office. Once inside the elevator, he grabbed the can of Copenhagen from his jacket pocket and stuffed a big wad of the chewing tobacco into his mouth.

CHAPTER FOUR

THE SUPER STOP AND SHOP parking lot was pretty busy, but that hadn't stopped Jocelyn from frantically cruising around it looking for clues. She widened her search for her children and had driven up and down the main street twice. Then she hopped on the highway heading to New Hampshire, but she changed her mind and swung around Providence. The car seemed on autopilot as it made its way back to the Starbucks located in the same plaza as the Super Stop and Shop. It was nighttime now, and she shut off her car and just sat, staring at the warm cozy glow of people enjoying their lattes. *Maybe I should call the police. They could put out an APB or whatever it's called.* She opened her cell phone and called 911.

"You mean the kids were kidnapped?"

"Uh, no. It's not quite like that. I asked him to take the kids, but now I don't think he's mentally in a good state of mind."

"Is he drunk?"

"I don't think so."

"Did he hurt you?"

"Huh? No. He did disconnect my power and phone but, look, I'm scared that he might hurt the kids. He's heading to New Hampshire. He's got a gun."

"Do you know where in New Hampshire he's going?"

"No. Can't you just tell the police to pull him over and take the kids away?" Jocelyn pleaded. "I mean, if he's really going to New Hampshire, he's got to be on Route 95. His license plate number is—"

"Does he have legal custody of the children?"

"What? I don't know. I'm their mom, and he's their dad.

Please just listen to me! I want my kids back!"

It was at this point that the operator had to calm Jocelyn down and began speaking to her in some sort of special needs/don't-jump-off-the-bridge voice, and that made Jocelyn start crying hysterically. The emergency operator explained that there was technically nothing the police could do unless Ethan was caught speeding or committing a crime. Jocelyn persisted and recited anyway, as best she could remember, Ethan's license plate number and gave descriptions of the truck, Ethan, and the kids.

She hung up completely deflated. She was furious with herself for offering up the kids to him and completely anxious that he might... he might... Oh, she couldn't even let herself think about it. She was just about to drag herself out of the car and get a sugary decaf mocha with extra whipped cream when she started tearing up again. She didn't need a coffee. She needed her kids. She shut the car door and just cried. She had never really been the type to pray before, but now she was crying and praying at the altar of her dashboard that her children, little Lilly and Will, were okay. That they were having a good time with their dad. That they both knew that they were loved, no matter what, by their mother. She was honestly beseeching God to protect them and bring them back safely to her.

When she had cried herself out, she decided to go back to their dark house and pack up some clothes. She was going to take Ethan's parting advice and stay with her mom.

***

Her mother lived the next town over in a cute little bungalow in an ocean front community. Jocelyn pulled onto the crunchy pea stone driveway and hauled her Kenya bag of sleepover gear up the front steps. She knocked before she entered, and her mom said, "Oh! Hi, honey! I didn't realize you were coming over tonight. I would have made dinner for us or something," while circling around the kitchen table to hug her daughter. "Where's the kids?" she asked, eyeing out the door, and that's when Jocelyn started crying again.

They sat down at the waxed walnut table, and her mother listened to random bits of the narrative overlaid with pathetic sobbing for a while and said, "Okay, once I get back from the neighborhood association meeting, we'll have some tea and really get to the bottom of it." Stunned that her mother was done with the conversation when she hadn't even got to the really creepy part about the cut cables, Jocelyn stopped crying and got mad.

"Mom! I'm trying to tell you the kids are in danger! I'm sitting here with tears in my eyes, and you have other things to do?"

"Sweetheart, I didn't know you were coming over tonight," Mom said as she got up to get her keys. "Don't worry, honey. Ethan loves the kids. I'm sure they are having the time of their lives!" She gave Jocelyn a kiss on the top of her head, snatched her purse, and was off.

Well, at least Mom's got electricity... Jocelyn wandered over to the couch and turned on the TV. She hadn't really watched TV in almost six years since she threw hers out before the kids were born. She was surprised by how dizzy she was becoming. The camera angles were all skewed, and the timing of the edits seemed much too fast. In fact, it seemed people were talking even faster than they used to. When she changed over to one of the news channels, she was genuinely surprised by how abrasive the tone was. Heck, even the little news scroll at the bottom of the screen seemed to be flying by more aggressively. She found her heart racing uncomfortably for no particular reason as she listened to the details of how the city of Tampa was gearing up for the Republican National Convention. She shut off the television and started leafing through the newspaper on the coffee table looking for the classified section. She had made up her mind. When those kids came home, they were moving.

CHAPTER FIVE

One week later
Tampa, Florida

MIŠEL GUJIC, TODAY ASSUMING THE name Missy Smith, glared at Heartbreaker. It really was sort of funny how the two female assassins didn't like each other, and that was probably why they were plopped here together in the first place. Missy could imagine Jonas Ledergerber chuckling at them as they fought back the urge to kill each other. Missy, outfitted in Walmart-purchased jean shorts, flip flops, and an I-heart-Tampa T-shirt spat, "*This* is what I'm supposed to be doing? Retyping faxes?" She flipped over the paper to see if anything else was written on the back. "That's it? I came all the way here for this? Are you *sure* you delivered the correct document? This has nothing to do with my area of expertise." She thrust the paper back to her companion with obvious disgust.

Heartbreaker, wearing a colorful 1970s-inspired spaghetti-strapped sundress, which left the casual observer wondering whether she had acquired it at a second hand store or at a trendy boutique in Italy, lit her cigarette and then casually proceeded to burn the evidence. "Yes. Is the paper," she replied flatly in her heavy Serbian accent as she watched the paper burn and flutter out over the water. When Mišel's orders were effectively erased, she took another drag off the cigarette and made herself comfortable by leaning against the balustrade fence running along the storm wall.

"Learn to speak English," Mišel hissed.

Heartbreaker squinted her eyes, calmly turned and exhaled all the smoke she was holding in her lungs directly at

Mišel's face. "You maybe kill the right baby-woman next time. No?" If they had been anywhere other than the heavily traveled Bayshore Boulevard, Mišel would have punched her. Her last target had been low priority, but still was the bane of her existence, really, and everyone seemed to know about it. Her most recent attempt to knock off the woman included concocting one of the most elegant custom blends she had ever prepared in her life. She had painstakingly pre-filled a month's worth of syringes, packaged them up exactly to spec, and the woman never even injected herself with any of it.

Mišel had been disappointed by this highly uncharacteristic behavior from the target. It robbed her of her glory. She had always considered her approach for getting a job done more civilized and refined than what her contemporaries were up to. Chemistry, to her, was more on par with some sort of high art or magic, and she prided herself for rising above the madness of messy stabbings or vulgar shooting. She was better than that—that was beneath her now.

That's because the killer who was Mišel (a.k.a. Missy, a.k.a. Shelly, a.k.a. The Temp) had been formed by her early experiences in the city of Srebrenica. The name of the place meant "silver mine," the same meaning as its old Latin name *Argentaria*, but there were gold mines there too, and zinc, and lead.

Lots of lead. Especially in 1995, after the Orthodox Christians had systematically annihilated over eight thousand Muslim men and boys in that city. It had been the worst mass slaughter to take place in Europe since the Second World War. Given that it appeared to be an act of deliberate genocide, the United States had aligned itself with the Muslim faction and then proceeded to violate an arms embargo, which only served to prolong the bloody mess.

Mišel had been among the nearly 25,000 surviving Bosnian children, women, and elderly who were forcibly transferred from Srebrenica, while the men aged 12-77 were taken "for interrogation" and held in trucks and warehouses.

The United Nations Peacekeeping mission was pretty much a joke. Luckily for her, after the body count reached 200,000 and NATO was eventually called in, she was offered an education via the humanitarian efforts of the Federation of Malaysia. It was there that she followed in her murdered father's footsteps, studied chemistry, and learned English from American English-as-a-second-language teachers.

Her smokestack of a fashion statement companion, Stojanka Davidovic, known to many in "the industry" as Heartbreaker, came from right around the geographical corner—the Serbian province of Kosovo. Mišel had heard Heartbreaker's story. Kosovo was home to a different war four years later in 1999. It was the first time the multinational defense alliance, NATO, had lashed out offensively in its fifty year history.

In Kosovo, NATO missiles were shoved down the throat of Slobodan Milosevic who was playing the religion card in his effort to turn post-communist Yugoslavia into his vision of a "Greater Serbia." Milosevic had aligned himself with the Serbian Orthodox Church, which promoted its own version of Serbian nationalism: a state in which Christ is the czar; the school where Christ is the teacher; the art portraying Christ as the magic; a place where slavery can be endured only with Christ. Et cetera. Et cetera.

Stojanka and her family were Orthodox, and because of the war and its hunger, she had embraced that "enduring slavery through Christ" thing as a personal mission statement. She and her sister had been bought and sold many times during the "Humanitarian War" by their entrepreneurial retired American General-turned-pimp. It had been a young military customer who had taught her to shoot effectively and to take her skills seriously. Her ability to shoot and kill with machine-like precision had eventually allowed her to leave the war zone and finally experience peace.

The very sight of Heartbreaker leaning on the balustrade wall of Bayshore Boulevard, smoking American cigarettes, irritated Mišel. "Jebi se, kurvo! How do you say in English? Fuck you? This assignment has nothing to do with me," she sneered as she yanked her duffle bag up to her shoulder.

"You are science specialist. You do typing," Stojanka offered as she continued to survey the lay of the land.

Mišel stared at Heartbreaker's profile for a moment and then turned and walked away without saying a word. She *was* a scientist, but she wasn't a meteorologist. Wondering why she wasn't tasked with something more substantial than simply a data entry position at the Weather Channel, she concluded that this was some sort of punishment for not getting rid of Jocelyn McLaren years ago. She begrudgingly strode off. The long process of blending into the woodwork began. Again. She would emerge when it was time.

CHAPTER SIX

JOCELYN SAT WAITING ON THE FRONT STEPS. She wasn't going to set foot in *his* house until *her* children were in her arms. During the past week, she had sold her gold coins at the place her friend Sam Ballentine had recommended; talked with the lawyer to whom her mother had referred her about custody and getting it all in writing; and put a deposit down on a dingy log cabin out in the woods. If the kids liked camping, as Ethan had let her know in his last phone call, then they were going to love the new place.

She checked the clock on her cell phone. He was already fifteen minutes late. She silently studied the perennials she had planted in the front flower bed and fought the urge to start weeding. Almost 6 years' worth of tending to lilies, roses, liatrus, catnip, phlox, iris, butterfly bushes, and a whole assortment of low-crawling creepers made her instantly feel lonesome. She would miss her garden. She got up and headed to the backyard to check on the vegetables, and that's when she noticed that the cables that had been formerly dangling on the corner of the house had been repaired.

As she stood there studying the wires, Ethan pulled up with the kids. She spun around and saw Will's and Lilly's happy faces as they pawed at their car seat restraints, excitedly trying to get to her. Ethan's truck wasn't even shut off yet when she swung open the back door of the crew cab and crawled in to hug them. She was choking back tears of unadulterated relief as she wedged herself into the rear seat of the truck, unclasped their seat belts, scooped them toward her, and kissed their precious faces. "Oh, am I happy to see you two!" she beamed. "How was it?" That's when she noticed that they were wearing new clothes. "Daddy got you some new outfits, I see." She was smiling at the kids, but inside she was ready to claw Ethan's eyes out. *Oh, sure, so you don't have enough money to keep the electricity on for a week, but you have enough money to buy both the kids Ralph Lauren sweaters and new L.L. Bean hiking boots.*

"Daddy got me my own sleeping bag! It's purple," Lillian excitedly told Jocelyn.

"Mine's blue," William added proudly. "It's warm! It's good for below zero."

Jocelyn continued smiling at her kids, nodded and exclaimed, "Nice!" and then turned to glare at Ethan.

"What? They didn't have any clothes packed, and we passed one of those designer discount outlets..."

"Do you know how worried I was?! Do you?!" she shouted at Ethan as she hopped out and helped the kids down. "Here I was alone in the dark because you said you didn't have any money and now… now this?" The kids looked confused, and Ethan looked pleased as he started unloading the cooler and the sleeping bags from the bed of the truck. She stared at him accusingly. "By the way, when did you have all that fixed?" She pointed to the wires securely fastened to the house.

"What are you talking about?" Now Ethan appeared as confused as the kids.

"The wires. They're fixed."

"I don't get it."

Exasperated, Jocelyn slowly laid it out for him. "Remember? You cut them when you left me here? Remember?"

"Uh, Joss, I really don't know what you're talking about."

"Bull! You told me you did. On the phone. When I called about the power being out. You said that you shut it all off. Remember?"

"Of course, I remember, but why would I cut the cables to my own house? There's master switches downstairs. I shut it off down there."

"There is? Where?" She didn't believe him because she had been down there trying to turn the electricity back on and didn't see anything that looked like some sort of master shut-off toggle switch. She was also irritated that he was talking about shutting off the phone and the electricity on her like it was no big deal. Mostly, she was pissed that he was dealing with her like she was a crazy person when she knew what she had seen. Namely, flaccid cables flapping in the breeze.

"Well, yeah. Come on. I'll show you." So all of them headed into the house. The kids were dragging their colorful sub-zero, professional grade, mountaineering sleeping bags, and Ethan had the empty, big red cooler. While the kids began busily spreading out their new sleeping bags on the floor in the living room, Jocelyn followed Ethan down to the basement where he proceeded to casually flip the electric back on and re-connect the phone line.

"That's it?" Jocelyn asked.

"Yup."

Her stomach did some sort of flip-flop and she sighed. Here she was in the dismal cement basement surrounded by random gun parts and his loading equipment. An enormous army-green gun safe was centered between two tiny basement casement windows, and she honestly began to wonder if he was telling the truth—as messed up as that was. She nodded and asked, "Then who cut the wires? I know what I saw, Ethan. I don't understand why you would do this to me."

Surprisingly distraught, he put his hands in his pockets and replied, "I don't know, Joss. I just... I just love you. Everything I do, I do for you. You and the kids." Jocelyn didn't even know how to respond to that. Some sort of rudimentary psychological synapse was short-circuiting in him, or her, or both of them, and she knew she didn't like how this felt.

"Ethan, even if you didn't cut the wires," which she thought was highly unlikely, "why would you think it was okay to just shut everything off and leave me here in the dark?"

"I thought it was the best thing to do."

"I see," she said carefully. What she "saw" wasn't making any sense to her, so she decided that this was as good a time as any to tell him, "Ethan, while you were gone…" She cleared her throat. "I... I got myself a lawyer and new place to live. I'm sorry. But I have to go."

He nodded. "And the kids? Are you taking the kids?"

"I got a lawyer for the both of us. We'll do up a visitation and support agreement. Everything will be legal. I know they're your kids, too, but I've got to get out of here, and I'm taking the kids with me." He nodded again. "I can't take this anymore, Ethan." She watched in surprise as he quickly wiped a tear away. She had only ever seen him cry once when the babies were born. She had not been expecting any of this—not at all. It was crazy, but the only thing she could think to do was hug him. So they hugged with the giant gun safe standing like a sentry behind them.

CHAPTER SEVEN

Washington, D.C.

TIM BRUCKER WASHED HIS HANDS and eyed his graying, receding hairline in the mirror. Being surrounded by the cool marble of the Congressional men's room used have a calming effect. But not today. It used to be so easy back when people were tethered to some semblance of a moral compass. He'd saunter into a congressman's office, all ballsy, with the pictures of the guy's mistress, and the next thing you know, the Conglomerate had a new contract.

Anyhow, it hadn't taken him long to figure out that he could easily be doing the same sort of thing for his own personal gain. Politicians usually abhor facing their own realities. Tim found they much preferred the campaign version of themselves and would pay to keep the lie alive.

It had worked like that with Stan Garfunkel, that congressman from Connecticut, for years. It was a weird sort of symbiotic relationship they had shared. It had gotten to the point that the congressman didn't even mind when Tim would show up threatening to expose his dealings with the government of Malaysia; or the ridiculous Chinese-made junk being sent out of country by the congressman's long time drinking buddy, much less the claims of sexual harassment. The Connecticut congressman would just sort of welcome him in, offer him a drink, and throw him some money while chuckling about it being the cost of doing business. Tim had begun to suspect something was up and that he was being worked around when the Conglomerate ended up buying that dinky little company passing off the Chinese-made stuff as an American-made Military Grade defense system and giving a huge payout to the congressman's friend to take a hike.

Tim did quite well exploiting that sort of thing for a while and in the process had unwittingly stumbled upon a new income stream. The intelligence community wanted him. They reached out to him in what he thought was a most unusual manner; but in retrospect, it made perfect sense.

The Council on Foreign Relations invited him to a meeting. They had members throughout the intelligence community and the media and were known to use a psychological strategy called a "limited hangout." A "limited hangout" is when a clandestine operation goes bad or a phony cover story blows up. When discovered, the operators volunteer some of the truth while still managing to withhold key and damaging facts in the case. Basically, it's a diversionary tactic; and if successful, the outed offender is sometimes rewarded for throwing everyone off track. Tim had been involved with former New York attorney general and governor, Eliot Spitzer, so he knew how it was played. Corporate crime information was lucrative and was a natural progression for him, seeing as he began his career as a bright-eyed and bushy-tailed lobbyist. D.C. was basically a refueling pit stop for corporations as they rolled around the planet, thus corporate crime and the management of political influence had become intertwined and his specialty.

But this thing with Jonas Ledergerber, it wasn't working the way it always had. The (nearly invisible) circles in which Ledergerber was moving didn't seem to react in the same knee-jerk manner as the political class he was used to dealing with. In fact, the more he uncovered, the more he wished he could run away and hide. He had never felt that way before.

He smoothed his hair back with his damp hands, took a deep breath and swallowed hard. He wondered if this congressman, whom he had never had the opportunity to meet before, was the next "limited hangout." He had seen how things progressed over the past thirty years. Maybe it was always like this, and he was just now seeing it. He opened the men's room door and headed down the long hallway to the congressman's office. How he wished it was as simple as the days when he was just blackmailing pedophiles.

The hall, with determined looking traffic scuttling by, now emitted a different type of aura for him. Just last month, he had felt as if he owned the place. But not now. The conversation with Jonas Ledergerber had made him research a lot harder than he ever had before. He had found himself sliding down into some pretty serious rabbit holes on the Internet, and he wanted answers, not money or favors. Answers.

He turned into the reception area of the congressman's office and spied past the receptionist, the dark blue walls, heavy white woodwork and red curtains that set the stage for the congressman as he worked.

"Hi there." A primly dressed, older than he had expected receptionist greeted him. "May I help you?"

"I need to speak with Congressman Pierce if he's available."

"Do you have an appointment?" she asked as she quickly reached out for the Daily Planner.

"No."

"Well, he looks pretty busy today," she said while studying the calendar. "Would you like to make an appointment Mr..." She looked up and held the pen in anticipation.

"Brucker. Tim Brucker."

She put the pen down and smiled. "I've heard about you."

Tim smiled back. "You have?"

"Yup. You are a Conglomerate lobbyist." Tim was somewhat surprised that this woman knew that. "Word gets 'round," she offered.

"I see. Well, when might I be able to speak with the congressman?"

"I'm afraid you can't."

"But I need to ask him some questions. It's very

important."

"I suggest writing him a letter. He's very good at getting back to his constituents."

Rubbing the back of his neck, Tim said, "Look, I need him to explain something to me. It's about money. I need..."

She cut him off and cheerily chirped, "Oh, he's written some books on the topic that you might be interested in."

Tim sighed. "Look, is there any chance I might meet him in person? To speak with him directly?"

"Not today."

"Tomorrow or any time this week?"

"Probably not." Tim rolled his eyes, and the unfazed receptionist simply said again, "Try writing a letter."

Tim nodded to the woman and left feeling as if the world had somehow just tipped off its axis mundi. This was the first time he had ever been put off like that.

CHAPTER EIGHT

Exeter, Rhode Island
Winter

THEY LIKED IT HERE in the log cabin, lost in the middle of ten acres that she and the kids now called home. It had been, like all of her previous places of residence, a "fixer-upper" when she signed the lease. It had been chock full of spiderwebs and mice droppings. The old windows were hanging at very wrong angles, and the refrigerator didn't work. But it had potential; plus, she had been kind of desperate.

With some hard work and regular visits by the exterminator, the place had turned out pretty nice. It was what someone with a healthy income and decorating sense might term 'Shabby Chic' because it was such a mishmash of decorating styles and what someone without might call 'Classy.' It appeared larger than it really was because of the cathedral ceiling rendered with century-old felled trees. Two huge, mostly white, abstract oil paintings that Jocelyn had painted dominated the far, rippled, log wall. Another wall was taken up with a 19th century cherry breakfront cabinet bursting with a collection of books. An elcgant antique club chair with swans carved into its arched arm rests sat across from an unassuming sofa. A small antique mahogany pedestal table, which had originally graced an Ivy League library, sat in a corner with a widescreen computer monitor perched on top. An enormous crimson oriental rug covered the wide plank floor, and lots of house plants over by the picture window completed the scene. The rest of the open space was comprised of a tiny kitchen and modest dining area.

Her mother rushed over to the screen door and called out, "Are you sure you are going to be all right in those shoes? Do you want to bring some flats with you just in case?"

"Nah. I'll be fine, Ma. See you in a few hours." Jocelyn hopped into the mommy-mobile, outfitted in something resembling what she might have worn to work seven years ago. A black pencil skirt hitting right above the knee and a crisp white, form fitting blouse. The shoes, in her opinion, made the outfit. She was wearing her four-inch high black wedges, but she didn't have any jewelry on. Ethan had given her a pearl necklace when they first met. It was lovely, but she felt weird wearing something he had given her to the State's GOP meeting. He was so anti-elections and government at this point that it just didn't seem right.

"Joss," he had said before she moved out, "why even bother? You know they aren't going to let Ray Pierce win. Same shit is gonna go down no matter who's in the White House."

"But someone's got to at least try to get things back on track. Stand up and say something. You, of all people, Ethan, know these wars have to end. The country is bankrupt, but for some reason we keep going to war. What are there? Like, three wars going on right now that the U.S. is pouring money into? Money that we don't have."

"Seven."

"What?"

"The U.S. is involved in military operations in seven different countries as we speak."

"You're kidding me!"

"No. No, I'm not. Joss, you are like the only one who cares. Most people have no idea how spread out the U.S. is and are happily oblivious. They don't care so long as a gallon of gas is less than a cup of Starbucks coffee."

"I think if people knew they'd..."

"They'd do what? Honestly, you give people too much

credit. They don't want to know. They won't hear it. They can't hear it. It allows them to go on living guilt free while slinging their superiority complexes around. Seriously." He looked at her with something resembling compassion. "Why don't you write a song or make art about it. At least that way you'll have something to show for your time. But these two political parties... I don't know why people even bother with these retarded elections. They're so easily rigged, it's laughable that anyone puts any trust in the process at all. You know it all comes down to money, Joss. You know that, right?"

Jocelyn was thinking about what Ethan had said as she drove off to the Shriner's Hall where the GOP meetings were typically held. She knew Ethan was right. At least about the fact that elections could be rigged. She had shown the HBO documentary Hacking Democracy to the book club, and that had blown people's minds. Turning into the packed parking lot, she decided to embrace cognitive dissonance and get in the game.

Even before she got into the building, she knew the wedges were too high for her. She hadn't worn heels in forever, and her ankles really couldn't handle it. She ended up hugging everyone in sight just for sheer support. People didn't seem to mind. In fact, the whole place seemed drunk, and all this hugging seemed to fit right in.

Smile. Smile. Smile. At least when she worked for the Conglomerate and would sometimes be forced to endure cocktail parties, she knew that there was some sort of reward involved for being mushed into a swirling mass of alcohol-powered chatter. This gathering of past-its-prime, vintage circa 1997 suits and dresses with complementing shoes was just downright depressing. Jocelyn tried to focus on her mission: get Ray Pierce elected.

"Look!" the guy at Ray Pierce's political training had nearly screamed at them. "No delegate just gets their name on the ballot and instantly gets elected! If you're dealing with a

Primary, the majority of the people voting are Party members. Get your face in front of the Party. Make them remember your name. Make them like you!" And that's exactly what Jocelyn was attempting to do as she paid for the tonic and lime at the bar.

"Hmmm... I could get arrested if people saw what I wanted to do to you."

Jocelyn turned around with her drink in her hand. "I'm sorry?" She smiled down at the cane-toting, elderly man who had just crept up behind her. "I didn't hear what you said."

"If I were a younger man," he said, grinning, "I would do things to you."

Momentarily grossed out, Jocelyn simply blinked and replied back with some comment about antique rusty cannons not hitting their target. The old man giggled and hobbled away as Jocelyn scanned the room for familiar faces.

It was your basic banquet hall with a bar tucked to one side, filled with your usual suspects trying to get elected, running around shaking everyone's hand. One of them, Harry Brinkley, had brought his cute five-year-old son with him over to the bar in an attempt to woo potential voters while getting his drink on.

Another guy, equally as egregious, was clutching to his chest, as if it were a Bible, a copy of Atlas Shrugged as he shook people's hands. Jocelyn surmised that some radio or cable personality must have mentioned the classic tome on their show and that Smarmy Politician Guy was proud to showcase the fact that he owned said book. The funny part was that Jocelyn knew quite well that this politician embodied absolutely nothing that the book espoused. That was okay because Jocelyn also knew that the people with whom he was shaking hands had no idea what the book was about anyway.

"Oh, man, you look great," whispered a familiar voice from the Ray Pierce meetup. It was Palmeri. Jocelyn didn't know his first name. He was just Palmeri. Everybody called him that. He slid up next to her at the bar while fiddling with an enormous cigar.

"Hey," Jocelyn sighed with genuine relief, "am I happy to see you! This whole scene is painful... What's that on your jacket?"

"What? Where?"

"Here." She brushed the shoulder of his blue jacket. "It looks like... like powder. What were you doing? Eating a doughnut or something?"

Just then a petite, smiley little woman glided up next to Palmeri. Jocelyn noticed that the powder on Palmeri's jacket bore an uncanny resemblance to the flesh tone of the woman's makeup.

"You've got to be kidding me," she whispered to Palmeri. "Dude, she's married."

"Who isn't?" Palmeri whispered back and proceeded to order up drinks for himself and his lady friend.

As Jocelyn looked around the banquet room, what had started out as a statewide GOP meeting began to take on the nauseating tone of some sort of over the hill swingers group. Palmeri was right. It was pretty obvious. She could see it now.

One woman, wearing a far too tight and revealing green cocktail dress, was pawing at one of the state representatives who was proudly showcasing his family on his campaign material over by the entrance. At another table sat two couples in their late fifties. One husband and one wife were clearly ready to get it on, but unfortunately they weren't the husband and wife who were married to each other. Their disgruntled spouses sat and sipped their drinks, trying unsuccessfully to appear as if nothing was amiss.

Luckily, someone came through and announced that the meeting would be starting in the next room, and everyone began the process of filtering into the conference area. Jocelyn didn't see Palmeri or anyone she knew. She did, however, see the clearly outnumbered Young Republicans, in contrast to the group she had just left, hustling around as if they were doing something really important. The chairs in this new room were set up facing a long banquet table where the chairman, the treasurer, and the secretary of the state Republican Party were sitting. Jocelyn positioned herself right in front with her 'I support Ray Pierce' sticker clearly visible for the benefit of those sitting at the banquet table.

The meeting went like this: The chairman got up and said quite a few words about fundraisers. A chocolate tasting party; a pig roast; a cruise on some really big private yacht that people would have to travel over state lines to participate in; and a yard sale.

Then the treasurer got up and gave a very dry overview of the accounting of the state Party's finances. Jocelyn was pretty sure she had heard wrong. The money the Rhode Island Ray Pierce supporters had collected and spent on campaigning, just in this state, was more than the entire holdings of the state GOP. But she had heard correctly and later realized that this lack of funds effectively made the state GOP the National Republican Committee's bitch.

Then the meeting was open to comments from the floor. Most of the comments were about the need to stop the current president of the United States from destroying the country via socialism. More than one person stood up and quoted, almost verbatim, something that they had heard on the cable news show *Hannity*.

All the while, the elderly, cane-toting pervert who had approached her earlier at the bar whispered sweet nothings to Jocelyn from the seat behind her. As the crowd was clearing out, the Geriatric Perv said something about her womanly figure, and Jocelyn, who had been ignoring him the whole time, finally spun around and said, "Look, old timer, I would slap you, but I'm pretty sure you'd enjoy it too much." With that, she wobbled in her too-high wedges to the nearest exit as the old man giggled.

As soon as she left the building, she took off the shoes and walked barefoot to her car. She felt incredibly empty.

Nearly four hours of her life had been spent on what exactly?

Jocelyn drove home. It was dark as she drove down the long, winding driveway to her log cabin. "What a waste of a night," she sighed as she pulled in next to her mother's car.

She felt badly that her mom had spent time out of her life to watch the kids while she was at that meeting. Fairly depressed and holding her shoes in one hand, she climbed the splintery stairway up to the entrance of the cabin.

"How was the meeting?" her mother cheerfully asked.

"It was horrible, Mom. Thanks for watching the kids, though," Jocelyn said as she hugged her.

"Oh, don't be silly. You know I love it," Mom said as she grabbed her purse and keys and scooted as quickly as possible out of the house. "Oh, and by the way," she called out from the porch, "a man stopped by and left those papers for you. He said he'd be back tomorrow."

Jocelyn looked down at the kitchen counter. There was a stack of *American Free Press* newspapers sitting there. On the cover was the now iconic photo of smoke billowing out of the World Trade Towers and a headline which read: 9/11 Was An Inside Job.

"Wonderful," Jocelyn sighed. "What kind of weirdo is gonna to roll in here tomorrow?"

CHAPTER NINE

A BRAND NEW RED CONVERTIBLE Corvette snaked its way up the wooded driveway to the log cabin. Jocelyn was on the porch with the kids when they saw it. Leaving the kids to observe the proceedings, she came down the splintery stairs and stood in the driveway to greet the visitor. A gentleman with a salt and pepper head stopped the car and waved from his al-fresco driver's seat.

"Hello!" he called out over the finely tuned rumble of his engine.

"Hi," Jocelyn called back and waved as she approached the car.

"Did you get the newspapers I left for you last night?"

"Yeah. I did. Thank you." Jocelyn was trying figure out if she had ever seen this guy before. He seemed kind of familiar... really familiar.

"I left a big stack. Hand those out to everyone you meet. Hopefully, people will get a clue and think twice about who the terrorists really are."

"Uh-huh." Jocelyn skeptically nodded as she continued to try and figure out who the heck this guy was. He quickly changed the subject away from 9/11.

"Look, you're going to be a delegate for Ray Pierce, and I thought I'd track you down. I figured you might need all the help you could get."

"Oh. That was nice of you," she said, leaving off '*I guess*' as she scanned the car's Virginia license plate. She wondered why he had chosen to say that she was going to be a delegate as if it were a foregone conclusion. The primary hadn't even happened yet, but she let it slide because she really did hope that she would get elected. "Nice car. It looks good on you."

"Thanks," the driver said without hiding pride of ownership.

"Have I met you before?" Jocelyn inched closer to the car. "You look sort of familiar."

"You don't remember?!" he laughed. "I guess my hair was different then." Smoothing his middle-aged, graying locks while looking in the rearview mirror, he said, "I worked with you."

"You did?"

"Yes. I visited your division on quite a few occasions and met with your boss, Robert King. I had heard about you before I ever met you." He smiled. "You and I were actually in a meeting together once in Virginia. At the time, I was working as a lobbyist."

"I'm sorry. What did you say your name was?" Jocelyn probed.

The man shook his head. "No. No, I'm sorry. I didn't introduce myself. I'm Tim Brucker. Remember? Mariam Stein had recommended you, and we all met at the corporate branch office in Virginia. General Vaughn passed out some book that he had done up."

It instantly clicked. That was the day Stan the Congressman had whisked her away for breakfast. Yes, she remembered. More pressingly, she also remembered with growing panic, that this was the guy she thought she saw at the International House of Pancakes. "Oh, yeah. Okay, now I remember. I guess your hair did throw me off." Back-pedaling because she thought what she had said might have been rude, she added, "But it makes you look more distinguished."

"Well, thank you. I wish my ex-wife would have thought that."

Jocelyn gave a little smirk of a smile. *What a player this guy is.*

The conversation turned to rehashing Jocelyn's memory

about the one thing they had in common—the Conglomerate and its board of directors. "Damn shame about Mariam. Who would have thought she would have had an embolism? She really was a wonder. She had a brilliant mind. I respected her a lot."

"An embolism?"

"Yeah. I guess you didn't see the notice? The Conglomerate circulated it, and it was in most of the financial papers."

"Seriously?" Jocelyn questioned, wondering how the FBI photos that she had been called in to look at of a gruesome crime scene fit together with what this guy just said. The indistinguishable woman in the photos she had seen had been meticulously sliced to death, probably tortured, had broken legs and was stabbed in the eye with a butterfly pin. The FBI agent had told her the victim was Miriam Stein. Were they even talking about the same woman? "Yeah. The thing I read said that she had some sort of sudden retinal embolism, and it made her go blind. Apparently, she fell down, scratched herself up and broke both her legs. She was dead for a couple of days, I think, before anyone found her. A really shitty way to go."

Close enough. Embolism/stabbed in the eye with a gaudy butterfly brooch. Yup, they were most likely talking about the same person, and Jocelyn wondered why it would end up getting glossed over. The only thing she could think of was that a miserable murder couldn't possibly be good for enhancing shareholder value.

"I'm surprised you didn't hear about it."

"Maybe I did," Jocelyn said, deliberately avoiding mentioning that the FBI recently gave her this news, "but I was on my way out." She pointed to her sweater-wearing six-year-old twins. "I was getting ready to have those guys."

"Cute kids." Tim smiled and nodded in the children's general direction. "I can see why you might not have had time to pay attention to death notices. Twins. That's a lot of work."

Looking up at her kids, who were shyly watching the whole scene from their perch behind the porch railing, Jocelyn added, "Yeah, and I homeschool them, too."

"Whoa. That *is* a lot of work! Good for you."

"Nah, it's not that hard. They're the reason I decided to run as a delegate for Ray Pierce. I can't have them growing up in this mess."

She would have gone on, but she really didn't want to expound upon the implications of the now outrageous, never-to-be-paid-off national debt; the fact that U.S. currency was now solely based on debt; the eventual loss of civil liberties that would ultimately follow the financial problems; the possibility of currency collapse; and the historic probability of desperate attempts at war to energize a failing economy—wars that her kids would have to fight, or at least pay for. She didn't want to get into all that with this sports-car driving, mid-life crisis in front of her.

This guy, if she remembered correctly, was a board member over at the Conglomerate *and* a lobbyist. A real winning combination! She had a hard time believing that he'd somehow become an advocate for Ray Pierce *and* the 9/11 truth movement when he had to be raking in tons of money maintaining the status quo.

This makes no sense. Why is he even here? Jocelyn wondered. It really did make no sense.

"I totally understand," Tim said. "That's why I came and dropped off those newspapers. People need to know what is going on, or at least start asking questions. Pass out those papers. That's all anyone can really do at this point."

Jocelyn stared at the man, whom she was beginning to appreciate as some sort of freakish mix of frantic and suave. While the rhythmic rumble of the V8 engine continued to drone on, she considered her words. "You drove all the way here because I'm running as a delegate for Ray Pierce? And to give me some newspapers to hand out? What gives, mister?"

His face fell serious.

"Ray Pierce will not win," he said as he cupped the visor of the black baseball hat that had been on the seat next to him. "Hell, they're not even going to let him get a word in edgewise during the debates. Just you watch." Tim looked downhearted as he flicked the hat onto his head. "Winning an election? Ha. That's not what Pierce is here for. He'll be lucky if he doesn't end up in jail. Believe me, they're already putting money aside for that. But he'll be fine," he smirked, "because he's not rocking the boat hard enough. He won't touch 9/11. Did you ever wonder how he knew all that stuff he was talking about during his April 24, 2002 floor speech?" Tim's tired gaze punctuated this question, and he grabbed something from the little nook in the center console of his car. "Forget about the newspapers. I thought you would appreciate them."

Jocelyn studied the change in Tim. He now seemed obviously nervous. He began neurotically tapping the can of Copenhagen chewing tobacco that he had snatched from under the radio and quickly stuck a bunch of chew into his mouth. With a fat lower lip he said, "Look, you're not going to understand what's going on here, but I need to give you something that is going to save your life."

Jocelyn literally gasped. The tobacco. The guy at IHOP. The guy on her last day of work! Her intuition had been right and she got mad. "What, like the stories about the World Trade Center that you left aren't enough?" she snapped sarcastically. "You've been on my trail for *years* now. I should call the damn police!" She was aggravated and just wanted him to go away. Then it dawned on her that this guy had not only laid eyes on her mother, but also her kids, and that was becoming increasingly disturbing.

"You won't understand," he almost whined. "I see what's going on."

Not likely. You didn't even know Mariam Stein was murdered.

"This is much bigger than you know. You're not safe. Not since Malaysia." Okay, now this guy had her attention. She continued to say nothing and stare at him with her best poker face. Tim's whole persona and facial features seemed to morph with the oral dose of tobacco. He locked eyes with Jocelyn and said, "Malaysia is where the connection is. Your congressman, Stan Garfunkel, and the late Mariam Stein. Mariam's Diamond Index project never got off the ground. That's because it was perceived to be a terrorist threat on account of her Malaysian contacts who happened to be strongly anti-Zionist. Stan had been focusing on these same anti-Zionists to push through the Conglomerate's deal.

"Jocelyn, you might think this has nothing to do with the United States, but I'll tell you right now, Stan lost that election because of his involvement with that crowd in Malaysia. Between the Diamond Index attempting to codify the exchange of diamonds and the Muslim banks that don't charge interest..." He shook his head. "Mark my words, someone, somewhere is itchin' to give those Malaysians the smack down. Stan was able to get out with his life, but Mariam wasn't so lucky. Look, everyone knows it was you who got that signature where it needed to be for Stan, and that made you part of their club. You were on the fast track if you had stayed on at the Conglomerate."

Jocelyn bit the inside of her cheek and was trying with all her might to correlate what Tim had just said with what she had learned at the FBI about Miriam Stein.

"Jocelyn, seriously, you were left gifts. Coins that showed the dates the Malaysians were close to outing the whole thing. He knew you knew—but you weren't who he thought you were. Too bad he was such a dimwit. Because of him, they knew you knew—or at least everyone thought you knew. There is nothing more formidable than a keeper of the truth, so you were handled carefully."

What the hell is this guy talking about? Who is "they" and "him"? And gifts? Those gold coins? I didn't know shit.

Hell, I still don't know shit.

"You could have been more easily disappeared, but..."

"Wait! Disappeared? What the...? Who are you talking about? Who knew who I was?" Her heart was uncomfortable in her chest. This guy knew what he was talking about.

"Robert King. Your boss. He thought you knew. Just like he *thought* he was supposed to leave you those coins. They were supposed to be for me," he proclaimed while pointing to his chest. "That guy is such an idiot. Seriously. He has a real problem, but he's gonna go far because of it. I'd advise you to watch out for that man, Jocelyn. I wouldn't doubt that he wants you dead. He's got big plans." He shook his head. "Here." He thrust a small, balled up wad of handkerchief at her. "Take this. I certainly don't need this thing, and it looks like you actually might. Take it!" Tim commanded. Stunned, Jocelyn accepted the thing, and as soon as she had, the driver of the red corvette added, "Make sure you have this on you. It will keep you safe. They'll think you're one of them." And without further ado, he revved the engine, spun the car around and immediately whizzed away.

What the hell?

Jocelyn took a glimpse of her kids up on the porch and began carefully unfurling the handkerchief she was holding as she walked back toward the cabin. As soon as she saw what was cradled in her hand, she promptly collapsed.

CHAPTER TEN

WHAT HAD BEEN TREES WAS now sky, and what had been her car was now her son's tear-streaked face. Jocelyn took a deep breath, looked around and realized that she had fainted. As she attempted to sit up, she realized that she still felt woozy. Her daughter was just completing a careful descent of the splintery stairway and ran over to her mother and brother. Jocelyn's first response was to comfort her children. From her seated position on the pavement, she pulled both of them in to her and hugged them.

"It's okay. It's okay," she repeated.

But it wasn't. She glanced over at the white handkerchief on the ground next to her. It was gently fluttering in the breeze, and keeping it from floating away completely was the Carlos Delohim jewel encrusted butterfly pin that had been stolen from her car on her last day of work. The exact same one, as far as Jocelyn could tell.

Her head was heavy, trying to piece it all together, and she started rocking back and forth while desperately hugging her kids. "It's okay. Everything is okay."

BOOOOOM!!!

She and the kids stopped the rocking-hugging thing and looked at each other. "What was that?" her daughter asked.

"I don't know. But it was loud," Jocelyn honestly replied.

The sound reminded her of the time she spent the Fourth of July in Florida. She had found herself at some neighborhood block party where people were all about getting really drunk and blowing off serious fireworks in the middle of the street. Jocelyn had never experienced an Independence Day celebration like that before and had been scared.

Fireworks were illegal where she lived. She didn't think it was very safe and stayed a considerable distance away from the pyrotechnics.

"Oh, don't be silly. They're just fireworks. It's the Fourth of July! Just relax," one of the friendly neighborhood moms had said while handing her some sort of fruity beverage.

Meanwhile, some inebriated teenage kid had gotten the bright idea to blow up a propane tank.

BOOM!!!

The explosion temporarily ground the party to an uncomfortable and silent halt. That was until someone started a rousing round of USA! USA! USA! and the laughter and fireworks stared up again.

That sound of a propane tank blowing up was pretty much exactly what Jocelyn had heard as she sat in the driveway holding her kids. Almost ten minutes later, while the three of them were pulling themselves together and getting comfortable back inside the cabin, they heard the sirens. It wasn't until the next day, at the grocery store, that she would find out what the 'boom!' had been. Namely, a Corvette undergoing some sort of spontaneous combustion not far from her house.

It was a mystery, the local newspaper announced. The unknown operator of the vehicle was proclaimed dead at the scene. Jocelyn quickly purchased the local paper and scanned through the story, which needlessly repeated itself over and over with non-pertinent facts. The one thing that impressed Jocelyn was the photo depicting the remnants of a brand new red Corvette still smoldering as the three fire crews and confused bystanders looked on.

That night, after the kids were asleep, she pulled out the butterfly pin Tim Brucker had given her to really study it. She hadn't been able to bear the sight of it the night before. It brought back all sorts of weird imagery of the FBI photos of Mariam Stein's murder. Tonight, she was far more curious about the thing and the circumstances by which she was now holding it. She set herself up at her computer desk with the pin, a cup of chamomile tea, and the newspaper story about the car blowing up.

Could I really be looking at a million dollars? Jocelyn thought as she searched the web for images of Carlos Delohim Jewelry. She didn't know for sure if it was a Delohim, but after that get-together at Sam Ballentine's office when that guy showed everyone pictures of the Queen of England and the former First Lady wearing the pins, she was pretty convinced that's what she was looking at. She looked closely for tiny pentacles in the filigree. Yup, they were there. And those antennae... seriously, no one could mistake those.

Still, it could be a cheap knock off.

Jocelyn wondered why someone, whom she had only met briefly, would drive all the way from Virginia to make sure she got this. What was even more curious was that the guy got blown up only minutes after she received it. And where did he get it? Was he the person who stole it from the car? She knew that she had lost the God-awful thing out in the parking lot on her last day of work. And why, if this thing was so important, not to mention ridiculously expensive, why would they give it to her as a going-away gift in the first place?

Like, whose budget did that come out of?

Then she thought about the gold coins that she had sold so that she could move into this secluded cabin. They had just shown up out of nowhere, too.

Tim Brucker said they were supposed to be for him, that Robert King had given them to me by mistake. What the hell was going on at that place?

Jocelyn decided to make a list of all the things that she could remember that were just plain weird. She tried to document everything in chronological order. The handwritten list looked like this:

-Nancy dies

-First gold coin shows up - Why? Brucker says Malaysia
-Pages of proposal log book missing and then replaced - connection to dates on coins?
-Malaysia signature thing - I have the emails on disc. But still ???
-Gets promoted by board member - we only shook hands
-Stan the Congressman - connection to board member. Malaysia.
-Spam emails through website???
-Second gold coin shows up - Malaysia.
-I quit and they gave me a butterfly pin
-Board member murdered and stabbed in eye with butterfly pin
-Guy shows up with butterfly pin that was stolen from my car
-Guy says Diamond Index and involvement with Malaysian banks ruined election for Stan
-Robert King thought I knew something
-Guy thinks Robert King was an idiot and had problems – well, yeah
-Guy blows up

Taking a sip of her chamomile tea, Jocelyn sat and considered this list. Clearly, there was some sort of connection to Malaysia. She realized that she should probably include the fact that Jerry Apario had told her that he had been humping around the world delivering diamonds and jewels, which were, of course, a key element of the aforementioned butterfly jewelry.

Oh, and that the division's server had been compromised. It was sending proposals somewhere else. Naturally, she might as well add that the FBI had documented her Conglomerate email address communicating with the anti-Zionists of the Malaysian government. As she re-read the list, she began laughing.

And there I was worried about helicopters! Sure! Why not throw some helicopters into this mix?! Stands to reason!

Enjoying the temporary levity of her internal sarcasm, it dawned on her that her computer blowing up, her cell phone getting stolen, and the mess with her medicine delivery might somehow be connected, too.

Jocelyn honestly wasn't sure what to do with this now really lengthy list. She drew some arrows and underlined some things, and then for the umpteenth time, re-read the ill-crafted local news story about the Corvette exploding. "I give up," she sighed.

It was late and time for bed. She double checked the locks on the doors and windows—especially the windows next to her kids' beds. Then, after she snuck a kiss on each of the twins' sleeping heads, she went downstairs to make sure the 2x4 was still wedged across the basement door. Finally, she tucked herself into bed. Her hand, under the pillow, was gently resting on a Beretta 92FS. The gun felt unnatural, and she couldn't help but recall how she came to be in possession of it.

"Take it," Ethan had said to her before she left. "You never know when you might need it." Jocelyn hadn't known exactly how to handle this parting gift, but Ethan had insisted. "Joss, look, you're going to be alone in the woods in that cabin with *my* kids. I want you to be able to defend yourself. That time we went shooting, you did really well with the Berretta."

"I can't take your gun."

"No. No, really," he pleaded. "I'm all set with handguns. I'd give you a shotgun..."

"Oh, for Christ's sake, Ethan!"

"See! See what I mean?! We can't even talk!"

"Fine! I'll take the gun," she said as she hauled another trash bag full of clothes onto the moving van, "but I'd really prefer help moving some of my heavy stuff."

Two totally different planets, Jocelyn thought. As she lay there, she kept worrying that she might accidentally flick off the safety and somehow blow off her own head while she slept.

CHAPTER ELEVEN

Saturday
Three weeks later
Warwick Public Library

JOCELYN GOT TO THE LIBRARY EARLY, turned on the lights in the big conference room, and started arranging the chairs in rows facing the projection screen. Soon, random people, some dragging "Ray Pierce '08" yard signs from the last election, started filtering in offering to help with the chairs. At exactly four o'clock, the latest incarnation of the 'Get Ray Pierce Elected!' MeetUp haphazardly convened.

"No. We are going to ignore everything the official campaign says. They totally screwed up last time. We just need to get delegates elected. All he needs is five states. Five states that have a majority of RP delegates and he's on the convention ballot." Jocelyn watched as Samantha Ballentine addressed the group from the front of the room. Those in attendance were basically the same bunch that had been meeting at Sam's office, plus another forty people.

"Yeah, I don't trust that Jessie Banton guy," Clint said, referring to the Official Campaign's manager. "He really irritated me last election. I don't know why RP would put him in charge again."

"Well, Banton is married to his granddaughter now," John P. said as he casually popped an organic breath mint into his mouth.

"Ray Pierce's granddaughter?" Dear Abby asked (she was called that because she always got her Letters to the Editor printed). When more than half the room nodded in affirmation, she exclaimed, in what was eerily reminiscent of something off a late night comedy show, "Oh, isn't that convenient?"

Someone from the back of the room angrily contributed, "It's the exact same crew as last election! If Pierce wants to win, why doesn't he just let those losers go and get some pros in there?"

The tone in the room was getting acrimonious, and Sam said, "Guys, it doesn't matter. Things will only get better when the average person walking around can tell the difference between a bullshit corporate style marketing blitzkrieg and a real candidate who knows his stuff." Jocelyn thought that statement might calm people down. It didn't.

"Oh, all right, sure," Forrest piped up. "That's bound to happen here in America... *not*! I say if we want to save this country—heck, let's make that the world—RP is going to *need* that bullshit corporate style marketing blitzkrieg."

"Are you kidding me? That would literally be the antithesis of Raymond Pierce, and it would disenfranchise his current base," said his good buddy, Palmeri.

Forrest, looking at him as if asking, *where the hell did you learn those new vocabulary words?* sarcastically replied, "What? You mean that base of Internet savvy young people who don't even vote? Gee, wouldn't want to piss *them* off." Forrest rolled his eyes and shook his head at Palmeri who uncomfortably played with a cigar.

Someone else chimed in with, "What if we did some serious highway blogging?"

Jocelyn just listened to everyone bicker about how this year's campaign ought to be different than the last one and fought back an 'I told you so' smile. "I could always pull out that marketing plan I did up four years ago," she said. "I'd have to update the prices and..."

Over the past four years, things had definitely changed with the core group of RP supporters. They had all been educated about how the political system worked, so they all now knew what delegates were. They knew the difference between a caucus state and primary state, and were thankful because they were in primary state, and they didn't really have to know the ins and outs of *Robert's Rules of Order*.

The most basic thing that everybody knew was that the only way to get Raymond Pierce on the ballot for the General Election in November was to have him win at least 15% of the popular vote in their state's open primary in April. This meant that any non-affiliated registered voter (which was the majority of the state) could vote for Pierce in the Republican Primary. This non-affiliated set was what the RP crowd was hoping to tap into.

It was up to the group in that room to spread the word. Most everyone had already gone evangelical in that they had no problem chatting up anyone about the benefits of a Ray Pierce presidency, from the unsuspecting grocery store clerk to their gastroenterologist. It was obvious that the official campaign wasn't going to be wasting its time or money on anything other than important caucus states that offered a ton of delegates. It was pretty well known that Pierce had Iowa locked up already. He was set to win that caucus. Only four more states had to produce a majority of Pierce delegates, and rumor had it that Maine was looking good, too. Only five states, and RP would be allowed to give a speech that would be beamed into millions of homes in America. Those five states would also allow him to be nominated from the convention floor. Those were the rules.

It was this political 'Hail Mary Pass' that sustained the supporters if, as the media kept relentlessly blasting in everyone's faces, Pierce didn't have a snowball's chance in hell.

He's unelectable. Only a moron would vote for him. Someone really dumb. Oh, yeah, and racist too, or is it anti-Semitic? Whatever. He won't win. Don't waste your vote.

Even as Jocelyn finished up her statement about her four-year-old marketing plan, she knew that if attempted, it would be futile. The current president, the one who people were accusing of being a socialist, had already announced that he had one billion (that's billion with a 'B') dollars in his election campaign coffers. Ray Pierce had the ability to drum up millions of dollars from normal, everyday people, but he did not have multi-national corporate support. And multi-national corporations and their wealthy human counterparts, as Jocelyn knew all too well, were all about enhancing shareholder value. Typically, they were not entirely concerned about the general welfare of the corporation's host country.

After a few more people got to voice their opinions, the meeting was officially adjourned. It had been less than conclusive, but everyone left with the hope that they could somehow pull it off without the official Ray Pierce campaign, which everyone had agreed was more of a hindrance than a help last election.

As one of the last people out of the library, Jocelyn walked to the parking lot with Sam and Palmeri who was accompanied by that same smiley woman with whom she had seen him at the GOP Swingers Fest. They all said their goodbyes, and she chuckled as she headed over to her car. She had figured out why Palmeri was slinging around words like 'antithesis' and 'disenfranchise.' He was trying to impress that smiley lady. When she thought about him struggling to say the NPR-popularized word 'machinations'... well, that made her laugh out loud.

It was cold and getting dark, and the pavement under her feet was wet and slippery. The library's parking lot lights were just beginning to flicker on as she unlocked her car. She looked up, remembering how magical that moment of hesitant illumination had seemed to her as a kid. Then, noticing her friends as they pulled out of the lot, she waved. She went to open her car door but hesitated. Had she just seen that? Or were her eyes playing tricks on her? She thought she saw someone stealthily sneaking behind a lone parked car a couple of rows behind her.

CHAPTER TWELVE

"IT'S PROBABLY JUST MY IMAGINATION," Jocelyn said to herself. She knew that she had been on edge lately. As she attempted to talk herself down from the anxiety cliff, she put her hand into her black canvas courier bag and reached around for the Berretta. You know, just in case. She blindly found the gun and quickly grabbed it inappropriately by the slide while hastily opening her car door. Flopping herself and the courier bag down in the driver's seat, keys and gun in hand, she let out a sigh of relief. She was safe.

That was until she realized that someone was standing right outside the passenger side door.

Oh, shit!

Jocelyn found herself fumbling around for a lock that amazingly was alluding her. The person at the door came closer. She finally pressed the right button and, *thunk*, all the doors locked. Now she turned her attention to the gun she was holding.

Think, Jocelyn! Think!

She put her hands just how Ethan had shown her. Then she realized that she had forgotten to check if the safety was on or off. Good thing she checked. It was still on. She turned it off and put her hands back into proper position. It wasn't like the range. She was all twisted up in her seat, and well, it just wasn't the same.

She heard a man's muffled voice, and her heart slid to her stomach. *Wait a minute! I'm in a car, and he's on foot. I'll just drive away!*

"Jocelyn?" came the voice.

She kept the Berretta pointed at the unidentified man with her right hand and attempted to turn the key in the ignition with her left. She was becoming frantic, but the plan made sense to her. However, this plan was easier imagined than done. The steering wheel was totally blocking her left-handed efforts from where she was sitting, and she hadn't anticipated that the wheel would lock up, preventing her from starting the car.

Oh! Right! Wheel lock. Once in a blue moon!

"Jocelyn. It's me. Open up."

Now in total focus mode, she put the gun on the armrest and did that random jigger thing to unlock the steering wheel. The man started knocking on the window. She got the steering wheel unlocked, put the key in the ignition and started the car.

"What's the problem, Jocelyn? Open up. It's me, Jerry."

Jerry?

She picked up the gun and scrunched down to get a closer look. She almost didn't recognize him without his sunglasses.

"Oh, for goodness sake! Jerry, you scared the shit out of me!" she yelled as she leaned over the armrest. Of course, she had totally forgotten that the safety was off. The gun was live in her non-dominant hand. Almost the instant she stretched herself out and reached over the armrest to unlock the door with her right hand, her left hand, somehow, pulled the trigger.

KA-BAM!

"What the hell?!" Jerry exclaimed. Then, when he realized what had just happened, his arms flew up and he started screaming, "Don't shoot! Don't shoot!"

Jocelyn, completely stunned, slowly flipped the safety switch back to 'on' and carefully placed the Berretta on the dashboard. It's hard to describe the various feelings that she was experiencing as she looked at the windshield that she had just shattered. She needed a moment to sort out what had just happened. She stayed absolutely still, staring at the puncture wound and the spider veins in the glass. However, with Jerry jumping around and then falling to his knees whimpering,

"Don't shoot. Please, don't shoot," Jocelyn realized that she may have caused more psychological damage than physical.

"Jerry. Jerry! It's okay! I put the safety on," she called out from the driver's seat.

"No! No, you didn't! You shot the window!"

"Well, I just did it now. It's safe. I... I'm sorry, Jerry. Please calm down."

"What the hell were you trying to do?! Kill me?!"

"Well, what where *you* trying to do?!" Jocelyn decided to get out of the car to deal with this. "Who goes lurking around a parking lot after sunset like that? C'mon! What did you expect?!"

"Not to be caught in a demilitarized zone! What the hell, Joss?"

They were facing each other now and both were taking deep breaths through their noses. Neither one really knew where to start. During the stare down, which was going on way too long, Jocelyn started wondering if her insurance would cover the windshield.

Jerry broke the silence. "You got a permit for that?"

"What are you? A cop now?"

"Just wondering."

Then Jocelyn asked, "Jerry, why are you here?"

"I couldn't find you. Did you move or something? I swung by your house, and Ethan told me to go ask Ray Pierce where you were."

Jocelyn let out an exasperated sigh.

"I found the Ray Pierce MeetUp group for your zip code—well, Ethan's zip code—and you had posted that you would be here. I would have just emailed you. I had your contact stuff on the ChemTrailTales.com server but it's gone now."

"What?" Jocelyn asked, not so much because of the loss of her contact information, but because she was more than a little disturbed by his process of finding her.

"The website's gone. The server's gone. My big sponsor

is M.I.A."

Jocelyn shook her head as if shaking sense into herself. She had dealt with this guy and his delusions before. "Jerry, a website being down is not a reason to stalk me in the library parking lot," she said deliberately, as if helping a child understand that it was not acceptable to be picking and eating one's boogers at the dinner table.

"Someone physically yanked it up and stole the server, Joss. The guy who sponsors me had a lot of files on there. Which is kinda what he actually pays me for. But I like to think it's because he supports ChemTrailTales."

Jocelyn rolled her eyes.

"Anyway, when I tried to call my sponsor to see if I could maybe get some money to buy a new server, I was told that he was permanently unavailable."

"Gee, that's too bad, Jerry," Jocelyn said through clenched teeth. She was getting really irritated that this whole drama was because of some website going offline. "I obviously can't help you because, as you can see, Jerry, I have to use the money I have to replace my windshield."

"Well, you're the one who shot the thing out. I'm lucky to be alive," he replied flatly.

Sensing a kernel of truth in this but not wanting to accept it, Jocelyn snapped back, "Yeah, well, that's beside the point, Jerry." She took a breather and pointed to the windshield. "Now *I've* got to pay the price for this whole mess."

"Well, if I could just get in touch with Tim Brucker, I know I could get some money. And I'd help you pay for..."

"Who?"

"My ChemTrails sponsor. Tim Brucker. The guy's loaded. He told me that he and a couple of his friends were sponsors or something for a Formula One race car. Can you believe that? Like who has that kind of money?" Jerry added, "But I think American muscle cars are his personal favorites. Dude's got beautiful, classic Cameros; a sweet Chevelle SS; a couple of Dodge Chargers; like, five Mustangs; and a few

Corvettes. Wicked cool guy."

"Did he happen to have a new red Corvette?" Jocelyn asked.

"Yeah. Why?"

"I think your sponsor is dead."

CHAPTER THIRTEEN

IT WAS GETTING COLDER. They moved into the front seat of the bullet wounded mommy-mobile to continue their conversation, and Jocelyn turned on the heat. As she recounted the arrival of Tim Brucker at her cabin, hearing the explosion minutes after his departure, and the newspaper story, Jerry looked as if he might vomit. Then, when Jocelyn relayed that the former lobbyist/board member had left a stack of weird newspapers and presented her with that crazy pin from her going away party, Jerry hastily opened the car door and puked on the pavement.

"Oh, my. Jerry, are you okay?" Jocelyn said as she flipped open the center armrest and produced, like a good mother, some emergency Wet Wipes.

"No," he groaned. "I'm dead."

"Oh, not the friggin' ghost thing again," she sighed. "C'mon Jerry," she said, offering him a Wet Wipe. "It's gonna be okay. It's okay."

"No, Jocelyn, it's not okay," Jerry said bluntly while wiping his forehead and then mouth with the Wet Wipe. "It's really not. I didn't know he was on the board at the Conglomerate. He told me he was a whistleblower."

"A whistleblower?"

"Yeah. But I started suspecting a little while ago that he wasn't really a philanthropist whistleblower after all." He paused, then said, "Shit. I knew it. The guy was a blackmailer."

Jocelyn just stared at him and didn't know what to say. They both sat in silence as they considered the personal ramifications of the charbroiled guy in the red Corvette being a blackmailer. There wasn't much to look at other than the bullet hole in the windshield and the discarded handgun, and that certainly didn't provide much comfort at a time like this.

"So why do you think you are dead?" Jocelyn finally asked.

"Because I've got the back-ups," Jerry said as if it was common sense. "And whoever he was blackmailing probably had some juicy, expensive secrets." Then, he added like some sort of afterthought, "Hey, wanna go look at the backup files with me? Maybe figure out who killed him?"

Jocelyn hesitated, not because she was concerned about looking through a dead person's files or because she had sensed that he was pathetically asking her out on his version of a date, but because she knew she'd have to get back to the kids soon.

"I can't, Jerry. I've got to get home. Besides, this," she said pointing to the windshield, "is freaking me out. I can't believe I'm walking around with a loaded gun. I think I should just call the police or the FBI or something."

"Oh, okay," he said dejectedly. "You can do that. But honestly, Joss, they might eventually solve the crime, but I'm tellin' ya, it's not gonna make things easier for you."

Jocelyn thought about that, and then something dawned on her. "Jerry, how come you didn't say you recognized him at the International House of Pancakes that day? He was there. Remember, I asked you if you had seen that lady he was with?"

He shook his head and frowned. "I've never met the man in person, Joss. I honestly don't know what he looks like in real life. I dealt with him pretty much exclusively through text messages and email."

"You're kidding me. Seriously?"

"Well, yeah. I never had to actually see him. We did everything online." Then, seeming to spring back to life, he said, "Hey! Before I forget, I got us something."

Jocelyn looked apprehensive as Jerry reached into his Member's Only jacket pocket and produced two small, brightly colored plastic items. Jocelyn hadn't seen anything like it since 1995.

"Are those... beepers?" Jocelyn asked while curiously picking up the neon green paging device and leaving him the neon pink one.

"Yeah," he said proudly. "I figured this might be better than us trying to call or email each other."

"Where the heck do you even get stuff like this these days?" she asked, slightly amazed.

"Gina and Gino's father," Jerry said blankly.

Jocelyn furrowed her brow. "You're still talking to them? Even after Gina gave you a concussion?"

He nodded sheepishly. "Well, not Gina. I'm not talking to her. Ever. Gino's cool though. His dad has like boxes and boxes of these things sitting around. Gino said it wouldn't matter if I took a few."

The beepers seemed rather unnecessary to Jocelyn, and trotting around with a neon green beeper that veritably screamed, 'Hi! I'm a prostitute and/or drug dealer from 1995!' just wasn't very appealing to her. Before she could voice her objections, Jerry excitedly handed her a folded piece of paper.

"In a pinch, we can quickly alert each other," he said.

Jocelyn apprehensively looked at the folded piece of paper:

65=OK	4357=help
4433=hide	786=run
326437=danger	4467=IHOP
66=no	937=yes

"Jerry, I can't even remember my own cell phone number half the time. I don't think I'll be able to deal with this."

"Oh, it's really simple. Just look at your phone. There are letters associated with each number on the dial pad. It's not hard," he said as he wrote down their beeper numbers at the bottom of her Handy-Dandy Secret Message List. "This is me. Just call this number," he said, circling what he had just written, "and leave a call back number. Of course, you *don't* want me to call you at home or on your cell. Give me a pay phone or something. If it's urgent, just punch in one of these codes. Got it?"

Jocelyn exhaled knowing that he had obviously put a lot of thought into this. "Okay, Jerry," she said, accepting the gift of the beeper that she secretly swore she would never use. "Thank you for thinking of me."

"No problem, Joss. I think we've got to stick together on this. Even if you call the police or the FBI, I don't think we can be too careful."

Under normal circumstances, Jocelyn would have thought this statement overly dramatic. But as she sat looking at the self-inflicted bullet damage to her car, she had to admit that she agreed. She nodded. "I'll call that guy, McDonnell, from the FBI tomorrow."

CHAPTER FOURTEEN

AS JOCELYN DROVE CAUTIOUSLY HOME, she paid careful attention to the expansion of the glistening glass spiderweb creeping over her. The stress of the highway wind caused what had originally been a tidy hole with some little concentric rings around it, to become your classic shattered windshield. Jocelyn couldn't see much through the cracked glass and decided to drive with her head out the window. It was really cold out, and she had the heat cranked all the way up. This is when she noticed that it was starting to rain. Clearly, there was no need to turn on the wipers.

Finally, she got home. When she reached the cabin, she figured her appearance was that of a homeless Category 5 hurricane survivor. She relieved the texting fiend, otherwise known as the overpriced baby sitter, from kid watch. The sitter didn't comment on Jocelyn's obviously disheveled state of being and eagerly grabbed the cash while making her way out the door. *Fine by me. I've had enough to deal with tonight,* thought Jocelyn as she watched the girl leave. She immediately checked on the kids who were freshly off to sleep and started her obsessive/compulsive lock-check routine. She was down in the basement confirming that the 2x4 was still firmly in position when she heard the knocking at the front door.

"Oh, brother. The sitter must have forgotten something," she sighed and headed back upstairs. All she wanted to do was jump in the shower, then go to bed and forget about everything.

"Yes? Better make it quick, my bubble bath awaits!" she called out jokingly, but she really did just want to go to bed.

Fully expecting The Texting Fiend to be on the other

side, Jocelyn swung open the door, only to reveal FBI Special Agent Dobson standing on her porch. His partner, S.A. McDonnell, was jogging through the cold rain up the splintery stairs to join him.

"Oh... hi..." Jocelyn said as she ran her fingers through her hair, horribly aware that she looked like a freak. She hadn't bothered to take off her coat yet, her sixty mile-per-hour windblown hair had some sort of wet leaves in it, and she had noticed, while passing a mirror during the lock-check, that her non-waterproof mascara was drooled all over her face.

Clearly baffled by her appearance, Dobson skipped introduction and asked, "Are you all right?"

"Oh, I just got home. I've been running around all day and then the rain came..."

"I see," said Dobson.

McDonnell muscled his way past Dobson. "What happened to that car?" he asked as he turned to point at it.

"Oh, hi, Special Agent McDonnell!" Jocelyn said trying to sound cheerful. "I was just thinking of you. Please, won't you both come in?"

They both accepted the invitation. "Classy," Dobson said as he stepped over the threshold and obviously took inventory of the interior of the cabin.

"Thanks. I've been hauling all this stuff around since..." she trailed off momentarily feeling the sensation of her Conglomerate life running through her. She sighed. "I used to live in a really big Victorian house. This stuff looked more at home there."

"So you moved again?" McDonnell strategically placed his statement. Unlike Dobson, he had stopped looking at her stuff and was focused on her. "You move a lot, huh?"

Jocelyn pulled a tiny leaf out of her still damp hair and looked at it. "I guess, now that you mention it. You guys want some tea?"

"No. No, thanks," they both mumbled.

McDonnell continued, "Last time we saw you, you were in that yellow house and you weren't too happy to see us. This time, you're offering us tea. Care to comment?"

"Well, I was going to call you tomorrow anyway. I think I need help."

Jocelyn didn't know exactly where to start. Then it dawned on her as she filled the tea kettle to ask them why they were at the cabin in the first place. It was after the kids' bedtime. Seemed like a weird hour to roll in just to say 'hi.' And how'd they know she was here to begin with?

"I'm sorry," she said, turning the stove on with new skepticism, "I didn't even ask why you guys came over. It's kind of late." And she added, just because she was feeling flippant after the day's events, "I hope you're getting paid overtime for this."

Dobson chuckled but McDonnell was all business as he continued questioning her. "Well, to be honest, Ms. McLaren, we're very surprised to find you here. We are investigating the death of one of Mariam Stein's associates."

Jocelyn was unable to suppress images of the crime scene photos McDonnell had previously showed her. The broken and tortured body topped off with a butterfly pin.

"Your neighbors reported seeing the subject's car leave this property just before his death."

Jocelyn nodded. She knew where to start now.

"The red Corvette?" she asked, knowing the answer.

"Yeah. The red Corvette. Wanna tell us about it?"

"Well, he came here the day before his car blew up and left these with my mom," she said, handing him one of the '9/11 Was An Inside Job' newspapers from the stack still on the counter. McDonnell took the paper, glanced at it and handed it over to Dobson. She continued, "He came back the next day—"

"Who and at what time?" Dobson interrupted while clicking his pen and flipping a page in his note pad.

"He said his name was Tim Brucker. And gosh, I don't

know. Around lunch I guess."

"And then what?" McDonnell wanted to know.

She told them the whole story of the red Corvette. All of it, except the part about Jerry and his theory about blackmail (since she didn't know if that was actually true). The whistle on the tea kettle started to blow. She shut off the stove and started making her tea as she told them her account in as much detail as she could remember. The experience of telling the Federal Government how it all went down was a huge relief. A rite of confession absolving and somehow blessing her.

These guys will know what to do. They'll take care of this. It's not my problem now. I'm safe.

She was just trotting off to her room to collect what Brucker had given her when something started buzzing. She stopped and looked around. It stopped. She thought it might have been one the FBI agents' phones or something. Shrugging it off, she hurriedly grabbed the butterfly brooch and nearly ran to show them. The buzzing started again.

"See? This was what they gave me at my going away party at work," she said, holding it almost proudly. "But," she said sheepishly, "I think it was stolen. I had left my car door open in the parking lot. That's the last time I saw it before this guy, Brucker, showed up."

"Fascinating," Dobson said as he took the pin and inspected it.

"I don't think I have to tell you that it looks an awful lot like the thing found on Mariam Stein," McDonnell commented as he leered over his partner's shoulder to get a closer look.

BZZZZ! BZZZZ! BZZZZ!

"Fascinating," Dobson said again. Both men seemed totally oblivious to the buzzing sound. It was only after she handed over nearly a million dollars' worth of jewelry and McDonnell distractedly turned the pager off for her, that the interview suddenly seemed over.

“So, uhm... that’s it?” Jocelyn asked as she accepted her neon green pager and followed both to the door.

“Yup. I guess so,” McDonnell said keeping one eye on the pin Dobson was escorting out of the cabin. “We’ll be in touch if we need anything else. We know where you live now.”

After she had shown them the door and fastened the deadbolts, she marched directly to her purse and dug out that little secret code note that Jerry had done up for her. “Oh, sure! Why didn’t you just give me a bunch of semaphore flags or one of those big naval signal lamps so that we could do Morse code!” she wanted to scream after comparing Jerry’s note and the dial pad on her phone. How was she supposed to know that the series of flashing numbers: 324 7278 63 48 36 668 8255 meant: ‘FBI PART OF IT DO NOT TALK’?

CHAPTER FIFTEEN

AFTER LEAVING JOCELYN AT THE LIBRARY, Jerry had immediately gone to Starbucks and gotten a quad caramel macchiato grande to sooth his rankled nerves. He had the memory stick on him just in case Jocelyn had wanted to look at Brucker's files with him, but of course, that hadn't panned out. He honestly couldn't believe that Brucker was dead and, more pressingly, that Jocelyn had almost shot him.

Still sort of stunned by the evening's events, he tucked himself into a corner under a very cool pendant light that looked like it was made out of melted Jolly Rancher candies. The jazz music surrounding him felt good as it splashed over him, and he tapped his toe while silently sipping his coffee. After the song ended, he set up his laptop and began clicking around the backup directory. He was surprised by the volume of documents living alongside his ChemTrailTales stuff. He had never made it his business to look *inside* Brucker's files and he didn't know what he was looking at. Then after a file full of random pictures of jewelry—pins and rings that looked like butterflies—he noticed something he *had* seen before. Kiddy porn.

Of course, being in a Starbucks looking at child pornography couldn't be good, so he slapped down the cover of the laptop. The reason he recognized it wasn't because he was some sort of deviant. It was because it was the exact same set of images that had graced the spoiled kid from Egypt's computer back at the Conglomerate; the guy whom he and Jocelyn had called the FBI to report the day after 9/11. The photos of children posed in various states of undress and the scenes of pathetic anguish were hard to forget. Brucker had them all conveniently saved as thumbnails in one enormous PDF.

Taking another sip of coffee and looking at the now closed laptop, he decided that he should probably sit in his car to do this. If he pulled up close enough to the window, he could still access the free WiFi if he needed it.

He gathered up his stuff and headed out to his 1998 silvery-beige-taupe-but-leaning-toward-gold Corolla, which he had selected precisely because the color was nearly indescribable (an important feature for any ghost seeking obscurity). He put the quad caramel macchiato in the cup holder, started up the car and edged in closer. When he was nearly touching the glass window of the coffee shop, and when he saw that the concerned customers inside watching him approach had visibly calmed down, he shut off the car and opened the backup directory again.

Avoiding the offending PDF file, he noticed that Brucker had ongoing contact with Robert King, Jocelyn's old boss, regarding the pictures of the children. Specifically about the 'platinum images' of the children under three years old. Robert was currently paying Brucker with BTC, or Bitcoins, the new electronic alternative currency. However, the conversation about these images was much older than the advent of Bitcoin.

As Jerry scanned the progression of Brucker's conversation with Robert, he saw something that made him stop. Jocelyn's name. Jerry couldn't quite figure out what was going on. The men were talking about "Krugerrand" and making odd jokes about the year 1984 and McLaren. And as Jerry read on, it became apparent that Robert thought that Jocelyn McLaren was somehow connected to Brucker. It also seemed Robert thought that McLaren was supposed to pick up and deliver something to Brucker.

Jerry had to backtrack and re-read a lot of what he had skimmed over. Was Brucker supplying the illegal images? Or holding Robert hostage because of them? It was hard to tell. He was fighting back the uncomfortable thought that perhaps

Jocelyn was involved with child pornography or blackmail when, much to his relief, he saw that the name 'McLaren' directed him to another file altogether.

The McLaren file was not about Jocelyn at all. It was about some sort of car design. A Formula One car. Jerry couldn't help but think it was cool. Lots of emails and scanned images of handwritten notes. One of the documents was just a list of names. There were several text messages about someone getting shot and killed. Another document mentioned $100,000,000, and the next outlined the specifics of Brucker's 33% cut of a $100,000,000 settlement. Another mentioned Rome's Postal Service having all the phone calls.

Jerry scrunched his nose and ran his fingers through his hair as he read that. He was surprised to learn that, in another country, the post office would somehow deal with phone calls. He found his macchiato in the cup holder, took a sip, and continued to study the document talking about $100,000,000. And then... *whoa.* 780 pages of a proprietary McLaren Racing company document which Jerry was forced to just skip through. It was very technical.

Jerry wondered who the other recipients of the money were if Brucker was getting 33%. His coffee had grown cold, and he needed to stretch his legs. He had been sitting for a long time.

He sluggishly got out of the car, and the customers inside the Starbucks were treated to a painful looking twisting and stretching routine.

Jerry was just righting himself from a hands-on-hips reverse back arch when he noticed the people inside the Starbucks moving away from their window seats. With his hands still on his hips, Jerry completed what would have been a textbook example of a trunk twist. He pivoted around and was surprised to see a black Chevy Suburban racing directly toward him and his parked car. It all happened so quickly that Jerry didn't even have time to take his hands off his hips. He just stood there and watched as the black Suburban smashed his silvery-beige-taupe-but-leaning-toward-gold Corolla directly into the Starbucks window. The duo inside the black Suburban jumped out and rushed toward Jerry.

"Oh, my God! Are you okay?!" Jerry burst out, probably thinking that he would be the recipient of a similar greeting. Instead, he got a punch in the face. As he confusedly dealt with his nose and stumbled to gain footing, Jerry watched the other Gentleman's Warehouse customer (a.k.a. the assailant's carpool buddy) tear open the Corolla's passenger door and grab the laptop. Knowing that the laptop—and specifically the backup files—were the cause of this so called accident, he ran.

Jerry ran faster than he had ever run in his life. Dodging the incoming and parked cars, he veered off to circle around to the back of the building. He spotted a row of three dumpsters and headed to it. Despite the fact that Jerry had lived the past six years of his life as a self-styled ghost, he desperately wanted to maintain his current mortal trappings. He grabbed the side of one of the dumpsters and jumped in. Of course, the guy who was chasing him saw this obvious hiding place and was quickly there.

As Jerry, out of breath, feverishly burrowed under the leaky bags of coffee shop trash, his assailant pulled an HK-45 tactical handgun out of his jacket pocket.

"I know you're in there!" the Assailant yelled as he slowed down to bang on a dumpster. "Come on out!"

Jerry froze, his hand on a sack of coffee grinds.

"Don't waste my Goddamn, fucking time!" Jerry heard him smacking on the next dumpster. "Come out where I can see you!"

Silence.

The back door of the Starbucks swung open. The Assailant swung around to see a rather effeminate young man in a red flowery button down dress shirt and a trademarked Starbucks' green apron storm out.

"Oh, for Jesus Christ's sake, Javier!" the young man said.

"Can't you see this is so not a good time! I mean, there's an automobile in the middle of the... Oh. You're not Javier. Who are—"

Thwuuuup. Thwuuuup.

The Assailant turned his attention back to the dumpsters as the Starbucks employee fell lifelessly to the ground.

"I'm not fucking around, Jerry!" bellowed the Assailant as he banged on the dumpster again.

Just then, the black Suburban that had rammed Jerry's car through the window pulled up at the end of the service alley. "Let's go!" Carpool Buddy shouted. "McDonnell's gonna be pissed!"

The Assailant, apparently frustrated that he had decided to punch Jerry instead of just shooting him in the first place, expended the last of his bullets by firing randomly into each dumpster as he ran back to the Suburban.

Meanwhile, Jerry was literally pissing himself while the name McDonnell was running around in his head. He was pretty sure that was the name of the guy Jocelyn was going to call at the FBI tomorrow. Still lying in the stinky sludge at the bottom of the dumpster, he reached into his pocket. The little pink beeper was there. He began to formulate some sort of plan. He needed to prioritize. First, he needed to get out of the dumpster and get to a phone.

He emerged like some sort of zombie from the trash and wandered back to his car. When he got there, he heard the sirens approaching, which seemed like an appropriate soundtrack as he surveyed the totaled Toyota Corolla situated partially inside of what looked like a rhinestone-studded Starbucks because of the sparkly glass scattered everywhere.

Jerry was amazed to find that his phone was still there. His keys were still there in the ignition, too. He grabbed the keys and the phone and headed to the woods and began repeatedly punching in the message from his own cell phone. This wasn't what he had planned, but whatever. He had to warn Jocelyn, like, now.

It was becoming a certifiably raw and rainy night as he headed deeper into the woods to resume his life as a ghost. The worst part was that he smelled of urine and old coffee grinds. If it hadn't been for the smell, he probably would have been able to hitch a ride or blend into a crowd better. At least for the moment, the woods seemed the best option.

Jerry tried to recall what he had learned in Boy Scouts, but the stuff about moss growing on trees and how to start a fire with a magnifying glass—heck, nearly everything he could remember—was totally useless in this situation. He decided that he should keep moving for as long as he could in order to get as far away as possible from the Starbucks. Plus, hiking in the dark through wet, thorny bramble that was slicing up his clothes and scratching his face was helping him hatch a plan. At least that's what he was trying to convince himself.

Finally, after what seemed like hours, he had to stop. He started building a little lean-to off of a large maple tree with random branches that he had collected. When it looked as good as it was going to get, he crawled into it. He curled up with his hands in his pockets clutching his nearly-out-of-power phone and the pink beeper. He couldn't rest, let alone sleep, thinking about who could be out there stalking him in the woods. It wasn't a bear or even the police that he was worried about.

BZZZZ! BZZZZ! BZZZZ!

The sound cut through the stillness of the forest and startled him, but Jerry perceived it as if it were a nice, warm hug. He pulled out the little pink beeper he was clutching. It read: 4467.

"IHOP." He grinned and began repeating to himself, "International House of Pancakes, Reservoir Ave, International House of Pancakes, Reservoir Ave..." He'd figure out a way to get there. He was worried about Jocelyn. Really worried. He didn't understand why they hadn't at least tried to kill her, too. He figured it was only a matter of time.

Suddenly, his phone rang and recognizing the number, he quickly answered it.

"Joss? What are you doing?!" he hissed with alarm. "I told you not to call from your own phone..."

"I don't think it really matters, Jerry. Do you know how pissed I am at you?" Jocelyn's staticy voice scoffed. The FBI was just here and..."

"Wait! What? They came to your house and you're still alive?!"

"Well, yeah. Why wouldn't I be?"

"Because someone who knows your McDonnell-FBI-guy just tried to kill me!"

"What?!"

"Yeah, and my car is smashed into the Starbucks and..."

"I'm losing you. Did you say something about McDonnell?"

Soon, their conversation was completely consumed by the static of bad reception and hyperventilation. All Jerry knew was that he had to get to IHOP. No matter what.

CHAPTER SIXTEEN

Back at Jocelyn's cabin

ONCE SHE HUNG UP with Jerry, she tried to call Ethan. He had a ton of guns, and he would protect them. Not to worry. But he wasn't answering, and when Jocelyn finally did get ahold of him, he was at an airport... in Zurich.

"Jesus, Jocelyn! What am I supposed to do from here?!"

"Well, when are you coming home?"

"I'm supposed to be heading off to France in about an hour, but honestly..." he sighed. "Okay. Did you memorize the combo to my safe?"

"Huh?"

"Remember? I gave you the combination to my gun safe the last time you thought some guy was pretending to be a cop?"

"Oh! Okay! Like this happens all the time!" Jocelyn nearly shrieked. "I'm asking you for some serious help here! Gun stuff. Your specialty! And you're flying off to enjoy brie and Chardonnay! What the heck, Ethan?!"

"You know, Jocelyn, for someone who is so into politics and saving the world..." His voice started to rise. "Look, I'm just trying to live a simple life..."

"By flying all over the planet?! I thought you were broke!"

It went on like that until Ethan gave her the combination to his gun safe (again) and invited her to take whatever it was that made her feel safer while he was away. Right after she hung up from that conversation, she had tried to call Jerry back to tell him that everything was going to be okay. She now had access to a bona fide arsenal. Jerry, however, wasn't answering his phone. It was going straight to his voicemail.

That night she worried about Jerry. A lot.

CHAPTER SEVENTEEN

THE NEXT DAY, A BRAND new white utility van slowly approached and lurched to a halt in front of the cabin. A heavyset man in his late fifties, sporting well-worn work boots, climbed out and started strutting around her Hyundai Santa Fe like he owned it. He was adjusting the waistband of his work pants when Jocelyn came bounding down the splintery stairs to greet him. They shook hands and both stood with arms crossed looking at her windshield.

"Ahhh... yeah. I was behind an eighteen wheeler, and I guess a rock hit it or something."

The auto glass guy that the insurance company had sent out looked at her with patent disbelief. Jocelyn was just noticing the bits of shatterproof glass that she had tried to sweep out of the car crunching under the guy's work boots as he spoke to her. "Whatever you say, lady. Not my department. So are you gonna be payin' with check or credit card?"

"Do I get a discount if I pay with cash?" Jocelyn asked.

"Nope. Those days are gone."

Great.

Because of Jocelyn's bankruptcy, she had no credit. And because she was now anti-bank due to her new-found understanding of the Federal Reserve and the fractional reserve monetary system, she had no checking account. After paying her bankruptcy lawyer, she had pulled what little money she had left out of the locally branded manifestation of the Royal Bank of Scotland, otherwise known as ATM Fee and Penalty or just Citizen's Bank, and joined a credit union that offered free money orders. Money orders had become her payment method of choice.

"Can you bill me through the insurance company?" Jocelyn tried to negotiate. "How about a payment plan?" Finally, she had to break down and just tell him the truth. "I can only pay you with cash or money order."

He understood that reality, but the fact of the matter was that he couldn't do anything to help her out. "You got a family member with a credit card?"

"Uhm, yeah... my mom. But..." she grimaced. How would she explain this to Mom? The frustration she felt knowing that only a few short years ago she was, on paper, a millionaire and that credit had been thrown at her like confetti, was really beginning to get to her. To add insult to injury, her job history on credit reports no longer listed the Conglomerate. The top grossing six years of her life were somehow gone. *poof* Like she had never even been there.

She had only discovered this fun fact about herself during Operation Easy Extraction when a potential landlord pretty much accused her of being a pathological liar. The landlord incident had prompted her to check her own credit. When she did, she found that it listed all the flower shop jobs she had ever had since she was sixteen years old. But like a gaping hole in her official record of being a productive member of society, her position at the Conglomerate was mysteriously missing. Disappeared.

So here she was, forty-two years old, and all she had to officially show for it was that she had once worked at a flower shop and was currently dependent upon her mother to cover her financial ass. It just sucked.

"Yeah. I'll call my mom. Hang on." She was begrudgingly heading up the splintery stairway to call her mother when she spotted a black 1999 Honda Civic EX with only one hubcap coming up the driveway.

"Hey! LadyLiberty!" Palmeri shouted from the car as he pulled up next to the windshield repair van. Jocelyn smiled upon hearing her DailyPierce username and headed back down to meet him. The repair guy gave a manly nod and continued fussing around with something in his truck.

Distracted by the whole scene with the windshield and her lousy credit, Jocclyn said 'hi' but not quite as spryly as she usually would have.

"You okay?" asked Palmeri. "We're waiting for you at the warehouse. Wc finished up a wicked cool sign, and we want to hang it from the parking garage. The one that overlooks Route 95." He studied her with concern. "Remember?"

With everything going on, she had forgotten about the sign painting party discussed at the recent "Get Ray Pierce Elected!" MeetUp. Highway blogging, which was basically hanging up homemade signs on overpasses, was a big deal for the RP crowd. Especially considering that the company controlling most of the billboard advertising in the U.S., called Clear Channel, was owned by a company called Bain Capital. This same company owned 850 radio stations with a reach of more than 110 million listeners per week.

Almost all of Clear Channel's primary talk radio stations were affiliated with Fox News. Most all RP supporters were aware that Clear Channel, through its subsidiary, Premiere Radio Networks, auditioned and hired actors to call in to their talk radio and other shows to pose as listeners in order to provide planned content in the form of stories and opinions. Shows such as Glenn Beck, Sean Hannity, Rush Limbaugh, and Coast to Coast are all considered entertainment and are therefore able to do this legally. So Ray Pierce supporters had to do something to get around this entertainment masked as news scenario.

"Oh... oh. I'm sorry. I forgot about the sign painting party. You guys did up a sign without me?"

"Yeah. It's sweet. Thirty by fifty."

"Inches?"

"No, silly head. Feet."

"Whoa! That is cool!"

"Yeah, we need you to drive it there, though. I mean, it's

folded as small as it can go, but still, it's a haul. No one has a car that can deal with this thing."

"Well, at the moment, neither do I," she said as she glanced over at the damaged Hyundai Santa Fe. "I need to get the windshield repaired, but I need a credit card to do that."

Palmeri got out of his car. "How long will it take to fix this?" he asked the repairman.

"I don't know. About a half-hour. It goes by pretty quick. I have the replacement right here in the van."

"Oh, then use my credit card, Joss. Just pay me back. Everyone wants to get this sign up today."

"I've got cash right here!" she exclaimed and handed him the folded pile that she was carrying in her pocket. "Thanks, Palmeri!" Jocelyn was beaming. Now she didn't have to ask her mother for a credit card. *Sweet!* And now, even more importantly, she could finally go fetch Jerry. "Hey, before we do this sign thing, mind if I pick someone up?

CHAPTER EIGHTEEN

UNBEKNOWNST TO JOCELYN, Jerry had spent the night in the woods sustaining himself with a scant assortment of early spring bugs and mushrooms. (At one point, he was sure God was talking to him.) This was until someone found him and let him know the Starbucks, where he had eluded death, was only about one-quarter of a mile away. The hiker, for reasons defying common sense, offered to give Jerry a ride to the International House of Pancakes. That's where Jocelyn quickly collected him.

Now, Jocelyn, her kids, Palmeri, and Jerry were all heading over to the warehouse to pick up the totally illegal, non-permitted signage. Hardly an issue compared to what she and Jerry were currently dealing with.

"Mom, something smells yucky," Jocelyn's daughter, Lilly, proclaimed, pointing to Jerry who was sitting between the two kids. "It's him."

"That's okay," Lilly's twin brother, Will, said to Jerry. "I pooped my pants once, too."

Palmeri looked at Jocelyn to watch her reaction. The newcomer really did smell like crap. Palmeri knew that a lot of these Ray Pierce people were a little 'different,' but whatever. The guy seemed nice enough and was willing to help hang the sign. That's really all that mattered. Time was of the essence. They needed to have the sign up for rush hour traffic to get the most bang for their buck before the Primary election.

Dear Abby and five other ardent RP supporters, aged eighteen, twenty-three, thirty-six, forty-nine, and fifty-four met them at the warehouse. Everyone, including Jocelyn's six-year-old twins, helped pile the specially folded blue thirty-by-fifty-foot Seachoice poly tarp into her Hyundai Santa Fe. Palmeri had the bungee cords, and everyone was visibly jazzed as they walked through, one more time, how the bungee cord thing was going to work.

They would all take separate cars to confuse the cops in the event of a possible high speed chase. (Palmeri's suggestion.) Jocelyn would head to the fifth level of the garage with the blue poly tarp, and the 'top team' would secure the sign with bungee cords. Then the whole thing would be unfurled to reveal simply the name RAY PIERCE painted in white Palatino font to the traffic on Route 95.

The other bungee cord holders, three floors down, would quickly secure it into place so that it wouldn't be flapping in the breeze; or, God forbid, blow off the building and into the traffic below. They had thought it through. I mean, how horrible would it be if the only news coverage RP got right before the election was because of an obnoxiously large homemade sign causing a twenty car pileup on an interstate highway during rush hour?

With Jocelyn's car in the lead, the sign hanging convoy entered the enormous and unusually complex parking garage. Everyone was fired up and ready to execute Operation Free Board. (Yes, there were ample references to Lynyrd Skynyrd.) It was all fun and games until Dear Abby couldn't find her way out of Level B.

Finally, after handing cell phones around and exchanges of nervous but friendly bickering, everyone was in position. Within five minutes, the huge RAY PIERCE sign was hung, and they all scurried like guilty mice out of the building.

After fifteen minutes, they all converged at the predetermined meeting spot, a dirt parking lot by the CocaCola bottling plant, to bask in the awesomeness of their handiwork, snap photos, and congratulate themselves. While all the post-hang yammering was going on, Palmeri's cell phone rang. He answered it, quickly snapped his phone shut and yelled, "Guys! Guys! You're not gonna believe this! My buddy, Forrest, says that some anonymous donor has a big Ray Pierce billboard up!"

Everyone stopped talking.

"No way!"

"Where?"

"Who's the donor?"

While people were chattering about the mystery of the anonymous financier of the sign, all of them hopped back in their cars and followed Palmeri's directions to the billboard that had just been installed farther down Route 95.

Jocelyn's cell phone buzzed. She had a text. She glanced down to see the word "EPIC!" just as she spotted the billboard.

What made it even more epic is that none of the other political candidates, in any party, had a billboard up in the state of Rhode Island for the primary election. Jocelyn, her car packed with the kids and Jerry, followed by all the other Operation Free Board participants, drove up and down Route 95. They tooted their horns each time they passed the billboard or the huge blue sign they had created and hung on the parking garage.

Eventually, they all parted ways feeling very satisfied. That was all that was left to do. They had gathered the signatures. Had done the labor-intensive and expensive direct mailings. Walked door-to-door shaking hands. Had plastered their neighborhoods with flyers and yard signs. And, most importantly, had endured State GOP meetings. They had each done something in their own way to promote the man and the message of RP. What makes this even more remarkable was that it was all done *without* the support of the national Ray Pierce campaign.

CHAPTER NINETEEN

JOCELYN URGED JERRY TO SHOWER when they got back to her cabin after hanging the sign. The smell of his homelessness was getting out of hand. Jocelyn threw his stinky clothes in the washer while he cleaned up and offered him a white terry cloth bathrobe to wear while he waited for his laundry. They drank tea in her antique shop of a living room as the kids ran around irritating each other with toy swords.

Someone was clearly trying to kill Jerry. There was no denying that. Now, after recounting both of their experiences, neither of them was eager to call in the authorities. In fact, they were petrified thinking that the FBI was somehow in on all of this from the beginning and that Jocelyn had handed over to them the one thing that Brucker had claimed would save her life: the Delohim Butterfly brooch.

"Do you think that's why Mariam Stein's case never got solved?" Jocelyn asked as she bobbed the teabag in and out of her cup of hot water.

"Uhmmm... yeah. Of course," Jerry responded. "They don't want to solve it. Someone there is part of this whole mess." He took a sip of tea and straightened his bathrobe as he set the cup back down. He was very conscious of keeping himself covered. "I mean, have you ever looked at the FBI's MOST WANTED poster for Osama bin Laden?"

"No."

"Well, guess what he was wanted for before he was pronounced dead for like the eighth time? Guess."

"Huh? Being the mastermind behind 9/11." Jocelyn said like it was a trick question and then added, "What do you mean 'for like the eighth time'?"

"Joss, look it up! The dude was on kidney dialysis! He was never in some cave in Afghanistan. It would have been literally impossible for him to stay alive there."

"Hmm. I always thought those illustrations of the underground bunkers the Pentagon put out were way too Hollywood," Jocelyn said, recalling the pictures she used to handle back when she was working for the Conglomerate.

"Exactly. Bin Laden was wanted by the FBI for some embassy bombings in Tanzania or Kenya or something. They had no hard evidence that he was even involved with 9/11, so they couldn't technically make a Most Wanted poster out of it."

"Well, then why was it all over the news? I mean..." She furrowed her brow. The phrase 'increasing shareholder value' was, for some mysterious reason, stuck in her head. Just then, a plastic, Chinese-made rubber lizard was hurled in Jerry's general direction and giggling tiny feet could be heard running away down the hall.

"Okay! That's it! Time for bed! Everyone go to sleep!" Jocelyn apologized to Jerry and rounded up the kids. After almost forty minutes of the let's-go-to-sleep routine with I-need-a-glass-of-water thrown in for good measure, the kids finally fell asleep.

By the time Jocelyn came out to join Jerry in the living room, he had shaved with one of Jocelyn's razors, changed into his clean clothes, and smelled really nice. Jocelyn smiled at him. Jerry smiled back.

"I'm sorry. Where were we?" Jocelyn asked.

"I'm not sure," Jerry said. "But it doesn't matter."

The silence of the cabin suddenly became awkward, and a weird shyness overcame both of them.

Jerry was the first to speak. "It's funny seeing you with kids. They look just like you."

"Yeah, well, I never thought I'd be doing any of this. Having kids, living in a log cabin. None of this was ever part of the plan."

Jerry nodded and scratched the back of his neck. "Speaking of," he said, "I was wondering if I could crash here till I figure out what *my* plan is?"

Jocelyn wasn't quite sure how to answer this. She knew that Jerry was a target and just his being there that night was very unnerving. At the same time, maybe it would be good to have someone else around.

"Gee, Jerry, I'm not sure. I mean..."

BZZZZ! BZZZZ! BZZZZ!

"What's that?"

"I don't know."

BZZZZ! BZZZZ! BZZZZ!

"Is it…? Is it the beeper?" Jocelyn asked in confusion. "It sounds like that beeper you gave me."

They both looked around the room. Jocelyn went over to the coat rack and reached inside her jacket pocket. Sure enough, it was her little green pager buzzing away with freakish urgency. She looked at Jerry.

"Did you page me?"

He shook his head. "No."

"You sure?"

"Of course I'm sure." They both stared at it as if it were possessed, and Jocelyn had the urge to throw it.

"Well, what does it say?" Jerry asked, peering over her shoulder. "Is there a phone number listed?"

"Yeah. 703 area code. Why does that seem familiar?"

"Hmmm... I think that's Virginia."

"It might be," she said, trying to recall her Conglomerate contact list.

BZZZZ! BZZZZ! BZZZZ!

The tiny green device was obscenely moaning and vibrating in her hand.

"Can we shut it off? I couldn't figure out how to do that when the FBI guys were here. I even gave it to them to try and make it stop."

"So they touched it?"

"Well, yeah."

"Okay, so now they know about the beepers," Jerry said as he easily switched the thing off.

Jocelyn felt horrible that she had maybe blown their cover, and she quickly responded with, "They wouldn't have known about it if you hadn't been paging me all night long."

There. They were both to blame.

"Let's just ignore it. Probably some weird wrong number or something."

BZZZZ! BZZZZ! BZZZZ!

It started buzzing again. Someone was apparently hell bent on getting through.

"I can't take it anymore," Jocelyn said after about fifteen minutes of it going on and off. "This is going to wake the kids." She walked over to her phone and dialed the 703 number.

"You know," Jerry warned, "you probably shouldn't call from your own phone. Whoever it is will have your..."

"Jahhhhcelyn!" It was the unmistakable vocal stylings of Stan her former Congressman. Jocelyn could hardly believe it. "Uhmmm... Stan? Is that you?" she asked while keeping her gaze fixed upon Jerry for support.

"Oh, beautiful Jahhhcelyn, of course it is I." His voice sounded older, a bit more tremulous, on the verge of elderly but just as flamboyant as always. She could easily imagine a sweeping arm flourish accompanying this grandiose greeting. "I have been trying to contact you since I heard the news!"

"And what news is that, Stan?" she asked, trying not to reveal how freaked out she was having this man call her on the beeper that she had stupidly shown to the FBI.

"Oh, let's just say that you are a very lucky woman, and I'm very happy that I have you on the phone. Just stay where you are." Jocelyn instinctively stepped away from the spot she was standing and grabbed Jerry's arm.

"How so, Stan? I don't know what you're talking about."

She kept the phone to her ear as she led Jerry down the

hall to the kids' rooms. The look of panic on her face was so intense that as she pantomimed for him to pick up her sleeping son, he didn't question it. He just did it. Cradling the sleepy child, Jerry followed her across the hall to the little girl's tiny room.

"Fuck you!" she screamed into the phone before dropping it and scooping up her daughter. "Let's go! We need to get out of here. Now!"

The kids were crying uncontrollably as they all raced down the hall in a mass of uncoordinated and panicky motion. Her son, as he unsuccessfully attempted to free himself from Jerry's grip, was wailing for his blanket.

"We don't have time for the blanket! Go! Go! Go!" commanded Jocelyn as she grabbed the car keys off the top of the fridge. But Jerry, who as a child was pretty attached to his blankey, let go of the screaming kid and ran back down the hall. "Where are *you* going?! We have to get everyone out of here!" she yelled over her shoulder.

Less than a moment later, as Jocelyn was herding the confused, tired, and terrified kids out the door, Jerry was back holding the fuzzy blue blanket. Before he could even hand it to the kid, they all ran out of the cabin and down the splintery stairs. Car seats were the least of her worries as Jocelyn literally tossed the kids into the Santa Fe before she jumped into the driver's seat and started the car. As soon as Jerry slammed the car door shut, she tore down the long driveway and fishtailed out onto the main road.

"Where are we going?" Jerry asked above the howling children.

"Somewhere safe."

CHAPTER TWENTY

SHE WASN'T SURE IF THIS was a good idea or not, but what the heck. He had given her the combination, and she figured that he wasn't going to be home for a while. They pulled into the driveway of the yellow house that she used to call home.

The kids, of course, knew where they were, and because they weren't constrained by mandated child seats, they instantly jumped out of the car and ran to the house. Jocelyn and Jerry weren't far behind.

Jocelyn fumbled around and attempted to unlock the door with the key she still had on her keychain. No luck. She tried another. Jerry shifted around as if he needed to go to the bathroom.

"I thought I had the key," she said despondently. "I wonder if he changed the locks?" The kids were still weepy but had calmed down significantly because they anticipated seeing their dad. Everyone crowded around the side door as she continued fussing with her keys.

That's when they all heard it coming. The unmistakable *whupppp whupppp whupppp* of a helicopter.

"Are you kidding me?" Jocelyn glanced up while working on the keys. She hadn't seen or experienced any helicopters in a really long time, and now, and as if summoned from the dead, here was one again.

Jerry backed away from the door and surveyed the night sky as Jocelyn continued her fruitless quest. Just as she was going to try a key that she knew belonged to an old ride-on lawn mower, she knew it wasn't going to work but...

SMASH!!!

Jerry had grabbed a rock and busted one of the little glass

panes in the door.

Jocelyn looked at him with alarm.

"That's no military helicopter," he said as he forced his hand through the broken glass and quickly opened the door. He waited for Jocelyn and the kids and then hopped into the house just as the searchlight started its deliberate dance across the lawn. They watched from the window as her car enjoyed a starring role under the spotlight.

whupppp whupppp whupppp whupppp

Blood was trickling silently from his wounded hand. Jerry wiped his brow and swallowed. "This doesn't look good," he said with a blood-streaked forehead.

"Tell me about it," Jocelyn replied without bothering to mention the blood. She headed straight to the kitchen and grabbed the key to the basement, which was hidden behind the refrigerator. Jerry came up behind her, followed by the kids who were quietly fighting over something her daughter was holding. "Follow me." She unlocked the basement door, turned on the lights, and released the familiar smell of Ethan's gun oil and the faint reminders of flood-anointed mildew. Now all she had to do was remember.

She stood in front of the army-green gun safe and bit her lip as the helicopter continued its ominous hovering over the house. The metal safe looked like something that belonged in a bank. It was about the size of a large industrial refrigerator, and it had a big combination lock centered on the front panel.

Think, Jocelyn! Think!

She knew there were three numbers involved and that Ethan had explicitly told her to make sure to pass zero each time. She also knew that she had to go around that first number three times.

Around three times. Three. hmmm...

That seemed to spark something.

The first number is thirty!

She remembered that all the correct numbers ended with a zero. With three leading to four, well, that was easy to remember.

And the next number is forty! Okay, now what? Three and four. Well, three plus four equals seven. Three-Four-Seven. Some sort of Fibonacci series with zeros attached? Okay, try seventy.

Bingo! It worked and on the first try! Jocelyn was pretty impressed with herself as she prepared to swing open the door on its large hinges. Maybe, if it was in there, she would borrow that shotgun Ethan had mentioned. Before she could open the safe and reveal its contents, she heard Jerry talking to her kids.

"Where'd you find that?" he was asking

"Under the secret rock."

Damn. She had forgotten about the secret rock. Jocelyn turned around to find her daughter holding a house key conveniently labeled, in her own handwriting no less, 'side door' and Jerry nursing his bloodied hand.

"Jerry do you know anything about guns?" she asked as she turned her attention back to the safe and pulled open the surprisingly easy to manage, thick metal door.

"Well, when I was a kid, my dad showed me some stuff. Took me skeet shooting and... Whoa."

The searchlight from the helicopter swishing past the basement window seemed an appropriate visual complement to what was contained inside the safe.

All were sitting and waiting like well-trained dogs:

Colt 1911
Smith and Wesson .357 Magnum
Ruger .44 Magnum
.50 Desert Eagle
SigSauer 226
CZ85
an assortment of AR-15s
a variety of Kalashnikovs
M14s

a Remington 700 chambered for 7.62 ammunition

Oh, and there was more...

CHAPTER TWENTY-ONE

THE HELICOPTER FINALLY FLEW AWAY, and she and Jerry decided that they should creep around Ethan's house and draw the curtains. "You two sit right here on this top step until I tell you guys it's okay to come out," Jocelyn told the kids as she shut the basement door. They started giggling, and Jocelyn opened the door. "Shhhh... and try and be quiet. Okay?"

She rushed over to meet Jerry and started checking the window locks and pulling shades down. Jerry pulled curtains together. "So do you think someone's gonna show up and knock on the door or anything?" she whispered as she hurriedly made her way over to the kids' room.

"Jeeze, Joss, I don't know." He followed her down the hall. "So, what did Stan say that freaked you out?"

She shuddered to even think about that conversation, it was so weird. The former congressman had been paging that number relentlessly to tell her... to tell her *that*? "First, he told me to stay right where I was. That seemed like a strange thing to say."

Jerry nodded and locked the window.

"He told me that I was going to be attending something important and to make sure I got all the details. He wanted me to make sure I told him all about it."

"That doesn't sound so bad."

"Yeah, well, he started to make it sound like I was some sort of call girl or something. Babbling about how wonderfully sexy my legs are and that I should wear high heels."

Deep down, Jerry wanted to say 'it's true,' but instead said, "He's been like that for a long time, Joss. You know that."

"Then he said, 'If your kids look anything like you, someone's gonna make a lot of new friends.'"

Jerry stopped dealing with the drapery and grimaced. "Oh, God," he blurted and rubbed his forehead. "But why'd we have to fly out of there, Joss? The cabin was probably okay."

She sighed. "Because he said that someone was on the way to pick us up. That they'd show us all a good time. To make sure I looked especially sexy. Maybe some fishnets. Fishnets, Jerry! He actually said that! Either he was completely wasted or…" she paused, trying to recall exactly what he had said.

"Jesus, Joss! Sounds like something right out of *The Franklin Cover-Up* by that Nebraska senator. What was his name? DeCamp or something?"

Jocelyn didn't even know what he was talking about, but her eyes started welling up. She was feeling very weak.

"Shit. I'm sorry," Jerry apologized. "Do you think that's what the chopper and the searchlight were all about? That they followed you?"

"I don't know," Jocelyn said as she tried to regain composure. She wiped her nose. "I don't know anything anymore, Jerry. All I know is that I love my kids, and if anyone tries to mess with them, I will kill that person."

After vocalizing that, she no longer felt the need to cry. She had replaced the confusion with a sense of steely resolve. She went back to the basement and opened the door. "Come on out, kids. Coast is clear." The kids came bumbling out and raced toward their room. As she watched them run, she noticed that the house was the same, but everything was different. It smelled different. The furniture was arranged differently. It actually looked better than when she had lived there. Ethan had painted some of the rooms and installed a wood stove. She was surprised by how sentimental she was getting about having lived there.

"So where are we gonna sleep?" Jerry asked while handing her a massive gun that looked like it had a tin can stuck to it. She just looked at the gun and then at Jerry and blinked. He silently placed it on the kitchen table.

She wouldn't sleep in Ethan's bed. But Jerry would. No problem. She would sleep in the kids' room. And because she figured that seeing their mom sleeping on the floor of their bedroom with a shotgun called 'The StreetSweeper' might result in years of therapy, she encouraged the kids to sleep with their Red Ryder BB guns.

Naturally, she had put up a fuss when Ethan had purchased the things as Christmas presents.

"This is so inappropriate."

"Yeah Joss, that's why they air *The Christmas Story*, a film about a kid lusting after a Red Ryder, every damn Christmas. Geesh. The next thing you're gonna say is that someone's gonna shoot their eye out."

Anyhow, her logic tonight was that maybe, if they were all sleeping with guns, it might seem kind of fun. Not so scary. Might be some sort of bonding experience... or something.

Finally, when the kids were tucked away in their bunk beds and lovingly cradling their carbines, she went to the kitchen and grabbed the StreetSweeper. Jerry had figured out how to load it earlier. After he showed her one more time what to do, she nodded. Without a word and armed with a loaded military grade shotgun, she headed back to the kids' room to kiss their little heads goodnight before crawling into Willy's blue, cocoon-like, Eddie Bauer Karakoram -30 degree StormDown, all-weather, expedition-grade sleeping bag.

CHAPTER TWENTY-TWO

ANOTHER DAY AND NIGHT PASSED with all of them scavenging for anything they could find in Ethan's cupboards.

"How do you prepare tahini?"

"What the heck *is* tahini?"

Despite the fact that Jerry, who had proudly commandeered a Smith and Wesson .44 Magnum, and that the kids all seemed perfectly fine sharing cup-o-ramen noodles, and with Jocelyn sleeping on the floor, she couldn't stand it anymore and announced that they were all going back to the cabin. She had her shotgun. Hiding out at Ethan's house was not cool or fun. They didn't all have to stay camped out there.

She wrote Ethan a note outlining, very briefly, that she and the kids had picked up a shotgun and a handgun and some ammo; that she had cleaned the house; and that someone was coming over to fix the broken window on the side door. Then she left what cash she had in her pockets for the random groceries they had consumed.

When all of them arrived back at the cabin, everything about it was the same, but something was off. She couldn't definitively put her finger on it, but she knew someone had been there. The kids and Jerry quietly followed her around as she inspected the premises. When she got to her room, she went straight to that little jewelry box. The one that she kept her insurance policy in. *Maybe that's what this is all about.* Her heart must have skipped a beat when she opened it. *Thank God.*

She was so relieved. The brownish-beige floppy disk containing the emails to Robert King about the Malaysia contract and the particulars of the forgery was still there. For whatever reason, she interpreted the presence of the disk as meaning that she was still "safe." That she had an ace-in-the-hole if anyone tried anything. She wasn't going down alone, even if she had no idea what the hell was going on. She refused to go down alone.

The rest of the day, she was obsessed with trying to figure out why she knew—like, knew with a capital K—that someone had been inside her cabin. The kids and Jerry, who seemed completely satisfied that everything was fine with the place, were playing in the yard. She glanced out the window at them. They were all involved with building some sort of fort and having a good time.

Meanwhile, Jocelyn was not. She was fixated on trying to figure the exact original positions of the tea cups on the coffee table when she heard a car coming down the drive. She braced herself for the worst, but it was only Palmeri. He headed directly to Jerry and the kids and admired the humble beginnings of their fort. Then he made his way up the splintery stairs and knocked.

"Anybody home!"

Jocelyn was glad to see someone from the outside. She had been cooped up with the kids and Jerry for way too long. "C'mon in!" she yelled.

Palmeri entered ready to comment about how that guy Jerry smelled a lot better than last time, but he got sidetracked when he immediately noticed the souped-up shotgun on the table. "Well, hey now! Is that a Striker?"

"I think it's called a StreetSweeper. At least that's what my kid told me. How'd you know it was called that?"

"I think I've played enough video games in my time to know this stuff." He had never seen one in real life and was fascinated. "Pretty cool."

"Thanks. I guess."

Palmeri walked around the piece with his hands in his pockets. "I'm pretty sure that I watched a show about how the

Israeli Defense Forces use this thing for riot control. I think it was used during the war in Kosovo, too."

"You know, now that you mention it, I think you're right. I have a book about defense contractors, and I'm sure it has a picture of one of these in action in Kosovo, Serbia," Jocelyn said, recalling the red hardbound book that General Vaughn had passed out during that meeting she and Tim Brucker attended. The meeting where she had unexpectedly gotten promoted. The same day that Stan the Congressman had taken her out for breakfast.

After many minutes of indirectly questioning her as to how she came to have a loaded, class three 12-gauge just flopped on her kitchen table and not getting any answers, he decided to congratulate her.

"Hey, congratulations."

"On what? This gun?"

"No, you won. Ray Pierce got enough votes to send delegates. And guess what? You're officially going to the RNC!"

Jocelyn had forgotten about the election. Politics was the last thing on her mind, let alone activism. In what amounted to less than a second on the kitchen clock, Jocelyn had experienced a millenium's worth of human nature. Specifically, that unless an activity directly affects a person's daily struggle, that person isn't going to willingly participate unless there is something in it for them. Before she even had time to form a real thought around what exactly constitutes 'personal benefit', because it's not always monetary, the fleeting moment had passed. She felt a twinge of guilt for not voting.

"Really? I'm going? No way!"

"Yup."

Palmeri recounted the excitement of the election night party, and Jocelyn listened with a smile. This is what they had worked for. But now... now she wasn't sure if she should go. Who was going to watch the kids? She hoped that Ethan could arrange his schedule so that he could watch them. He would be her first choice. Not just because he was their dad, but because she knew he'd protect them from whatever it was she was fearing.

As Palmeri rambled on with the election night play by play, the kids and Jerry came bounding into the house. Their fort was done, and they wanted to show Mom. They all headed over to the fort to check it out.

"Jerry says that it's just like the one *he* slept in the other night," her daughter said proudly.

"Nice," said Palmeri and gave Jocelyn the wiggly eyebrow, which pretty much shouted 'so-you're-sleeping-with-a-homeless-guy.' Jocelyn smirked and shook her head.

They all said their goodbyes, and that evening, after everyone hungrily devoured a real meal, she decided to indulge her curiosity about the StreetSweeper/Striker. She knew there was a picture of one of the Conglomerate's defense contractors using it in that book General Vaughn had given her. She wandered up to her bookcase and carefully opened the glass cabinet. The smell of old paper and ink invited her to take her time as she perused her collection.

"Ah, there it is." The red book was firmly wedged between others which related to warfare and U.S. history. She nonchalantly flipped through the pages. There. There was the picture she remembered. A guy in khaki pants, a black baseball hat, T-shirt, and terminator-style sunglasses was laying doom with a gun that looked just like the thing she had sitting right in front of her.

I can't believe I used to work at that place.

A feeling of bizarre nostalgia came over her. She looked at the dedications page where she knew she would find the name of the salesman who dealt specifically with the Pentagon. *Yup. What a life.*

After finishing her five-minute tour of the bought-and-paid-for literary infomercial... *What? It can't be...* She looked again at the picture of the StreetSweeper and then flipped back to the copyright. It was not her book! She closed the cover and looked at it. Turned it over in her hand. Flipped though the pictures she recognized. They were all there. She opened to the copyright page again, just in case she had missed something.

The copyright printed in the book she was holding was three years *after* her kids had been born. *Where the heck did this come from?*

With a sick sort of gratification upon realizing that she had been right, she now knew that someone had been in the cabin.

CHAPTER TWENTY-THREE

A few days later
Ethan's kitchen

"YOU MEAN TO TELL ME that this all boils down to Satanists and pedophiles? What is this? A sick joke? Shut the hell up. Seriously. Just shut up." Ethan had heard enough. "Look, it wasn't bad enough that I came home to not a crumb in the house and a broken window. No. The worst part was hearing from the kids that Jerry, the jerk-off IT guy, had been sleeping in my bed with... with my Smith and Wesson! And just when I'm thinking 'what could be worse?' you roll in here spouting off about this!"

"But that brooch, Ethan. It has tiny little pentacles on it." Jocelyn wouldn't let it end. "You know, the one they gave me at the party? This guy in a red Corvette showed up and re-gave it to me. The FBI took it and..."

"Jocelyn! Just calm down. Look, Mimi was probably throwing the thing out, and you ended up with that piece of trash. Seriously, you think too much..."

"It's worth a million dollars."

That seemed to shut Ethan up for about a second. His silence encouraged her ramble on. Trying to tie it all together was really hard, and she knew that she sounded like a freak. But it was *real,* God damn it!

"Jocelyn, if they were so fucking bad ass, then you and your new boyfriend would already be dead. You realize that, don't you?"

"First off, he's not my boyfriend."

"Whatever."

"Second off, I'm not saying that I know why all this is

happening. I'm trying to tell you that I'm scared. Mostly, I'm scared for our kids, and you're their dad, and I want you to protect them."

"Protect them from what exactly, Jocelyn?"

"Well, Robert King was in on it, and one of the Conglomerate's board members well, make that two—they're both dead. And of course Nancy. Remember, she did up the proposals? She died. And then Stan..."

"Right. And are you personally in possession of any real evidence?"

"Uhm... Jerry had some stuff on his ChemTrailTales server and well, uhm… It got stolen."

"So the answer is no. Let me repeat that, Jocelyn. You have no evidence! That asshole Jerry has you running around like a complete lunatic. Stop! Okay? Just stop! Tell that moron to take a hike! I'm pretty sure your sense of well-being will improve when he's officially out of the picture."

After everything she had just lived through, Jocelyn's bottom lip was quivering, she was so frustrated.

"Fine!"

Ethan nodded. "Good," he said as if it were the deciding punch. "You know I would do anything for these kids, Joss. Anything. And I'll always love you, too, but you're crazy."

By this point in their relationship, Jocelyn had been called crazy plenty of times by Ethan, but somehow it still bothered her. She fought back the urge to say something really inflammatory that would have just kept the fight thundering, but today was not her day to prove that she was right. After all these years with him, she knew how to pick her battles.

"I know you'd do anything for the kids. I know that."

He grunted and said, "You're going to be fine, Joss. Just relax. You didn't do anything. You said it yourself. There is no evidence. No one is out to get you. It's okay."

Although she knew that he still thought she was batshit crazy, it felt good to hear those words, especially from him, and she did calm down. She thought now would be as good a time as any to bring up where the kids would be staying.

"Look, I don't know if you know, but while you were away, I got elected to go to the RNC to represent Ray Pierce and..."

"Oh, for shit's sake, Jocelyn!" He threw up his hands. "You really don't get it. It doesn't matter. Even if everyone in America got off their ass, stood in line for four hours and voted for him, guess what? He still wouldn't get elected. There is way too much money at stake. And when I say money, I mean as in the whole world's financial system, for him to be allowed to win the Presidency. It's all about the money!" He paused. "Just keep issuing EBT cards and keep the stock market pumped up, and everyone looks at their 401K and thinks life's good."

"Well, I got elected."

"That's different."

"No, it's not," Jocelyn protested.

"Yes, it is. You getting elected to participate in one of the money parties' televised events is like that old guy with an oxygen tank who wins the slots at the casino. All the lights start flashing, and bells and whistles go off. It encourages everyone to keep gambling. To keep putting their money and time into the machine. They have to let some poor bastard win every once in a while. It's small change to those assholes. They probably write it off as a marketing expense.

"You getting elected, Jocelyn... you are being used. Hanging around on street corners, jumping around and waving to people holding a politician's yard sign. You are just an extra in their production. The whole thing is a marketing scheme to keep their game going. It's a *game,* Jocelyn. And it's fixed. Just like a casino. Imagine what would happen if no one participated in the game? Or, God forbid, someone exposed it to be the completely rigged pastime of some enormously wealthy and powerful men who consider themselves kings."

She wanted to say something like, 'you sound like a friggin' conspiracy theorist.' Instead, she said, "So, you think you can watch the kids for the week while I'm there?"

Ultimately, he half-heartedly agreed, and she gave him a money order for the window repairman. As he watched her back out of the driveway, he pulled the dictation pen out of his pocket and turned it off. Then he set to work packaging it up with the red book. The book that had, until very recently, graced Jocelyn's antique bookshelf.

CHAPTER TWENTY-FOUR

WHEN JOCELYN HAD HEARD from Palmeri that she was officially a delegate, she had been thrilled to receive a phone call from the State Chairman. She had lots of questions and let him know that she was really excited to participate in the election process. That she had been watching clips from previous Presidential Conventions and...

"Oh, it's not going to be like that," he almost laughed at her. "It's basically a coronation. A big party. You might like to go shopping with the other wives that week."

The wives? Who would spend all that money to fly down on such an expensive flight just to go shopping? "You mean the wives, who are delegates, go shopping?"

"Or to the beach. I'm in charge of setting up the speakers that are going to come talk to us at breakfast as well as coordinating the cocktail parties in the evening. Some states throw their parties during the mid-day recess..."

He rambled on with the various excuses he had for not hosting the most awesome party ever. In fact, compared to what he was describing coming out of Texas and California, his efforts seemed on a par with a Super Bowl party that didn't even have access to a television.

"...and I sent you a delegate questionnaire. Did you send that back yet?"

Honestly, the piece of paper that he was referring to looked like the product of a free Senior Center class entitled *'Mastering MS Word'* and/or *'Typing? Yes, you can!'* It was just a list of questions. (Well, not really questions technically, but the list included lots of question marks.)

Professional Background?

Hobbies?
Pets?
Foreign Language?
Fun Fact About You?

Each item was followed by a series of hyphens. (Not a straight line mind you. Hyphens with little spaces in between. Like someone didn't know how to hold down the shift key.) This was where a delegate was supposed to write their name, address and telephone number. All of which Jocelyn would have happily done until she saw the last series of hyphens asking her to list her social security account number. Someone had cut and pasted the GOP logo to the top of the whole thing.

See, this combination of questions and asking for the social security number didn't sit right with Jocelyn. They should have just asked for a list of her passwords directly, but she'd figure out how to handle this.

"Oh, I have it right here," she said, feeling efficient. "But I didn't really didn't want to send my social security number in to some mystery person. You know, identity theft and all. I figured that I would just tell whoever it was that needed it in person."

"Well, you can tell me your social security number right now, over the phone. I have to get everyone's social in for the Secret Service background checks. They won't let you into the conference center without passing three levels of clearance. Those other questions aren't really important."

Three levels of clearance? What's that all about? "Well, I used to have clearance when I worked for the Conglomerate. I'm pretty sure I won't have issues getting clearance to go as a publicly elected representative."

"This is for the Secret Service, Jocelyn. It's different than the clearance you used to have."

"Oh. So it's just you who's going to see this? And you're going to deliver it directly to the Secret Service?

The exasperated chairman said, "Well, no actually. I'm passing everything on to our friends in D.C. The lawyers for thc RNC will deal with all of the delegate information in one large batch, I guess. That's why they need everything so soon. It takes a long time to check everyone out. Just give it to me, Jocelyn."

Okay, right there. Red Flag. Jocelyn knew that the social security number was basically the golden fleece of the marketing world. There was a ton of important information that could be gleaned from a list of social security numbers. Add zip codes and *voila!* Marketing magic happens! Dark magic if left in the wrong hands, never mind the hands of a political machine like the Republican National Committee and its various subsidiaries. *Yikes!* Honestly, credit scores would be the very last thing on their minds.

It was just because of that that she didn't want to do it. She had already convinced herself that she wasn't so concerned about anyone seeing her bankruptcy or the fact that the only thing listed on her credit report was a flower shop job.

"Uhmmm... I'll give you my paperwork Friday when I see you at the Ivy League Alumni Club."

The next day, Jocelyn made it her business to sit in the waiting room at the local Social Security office where three people gathered around to skeptically look at the elephant logo cut and pasted to the document.

"Do they have the right to ask me for my social security number?"

"They have the right to ask you anything they want," said a full-figured black woman who looked as if she had just caught a whiff of some rotten milk. "But no one says you have to answer."

Then Jocelyn hopped into the Santa Fe and headed over to the Secret Service office. It was inside the court house building and not far from the FBI office.

She had to wait in the foyer of the building with a bunch of disgruntled people until they called her number. Then she emptied her pockets. Put her purse on the baggage scanner, which was proudly sporting the Conglomerate's logo, and walked through a metal detector. She was amazed at how the security had changed at the Court House since her bankruptcy appearance.

"I'm here to give my social security number, fingerprints, and whatever else you need for admittance to the RNC!" she shouted at the bulletproof window at the reception desk.

The middle-aged receptionist looked at her like she was some sort of crazy person, pressed the little microphone button and said, "Excuse me?"

"I was elected to go to the RNC!" Jocelyn paused, looking for a glimmer of recognition. When none came, she continued, "And the party wants my social security number for a background check! I didn't want to do it over the phone!"

The receptionist pressed the little button again and said, "Let me get someone out here to talk with you." She moved away while keeping her eyes on Jocelyn. "You can take a seat over in the waiting area." Jocelyn barely heard her but understood fully because of the pointing and pantomime.

She spent many minutes studying the framed photographs and a poster illustrating the evolution of the insignia of the organization. Jocelyn was quite surprised to learn that the Secret Service, until 2003 when it got absorbed into the Department of Homeland Security, was actually a branch of the Department of the Treasury.

How interesting.

For whatever reason, the sound of Ethan's voice saying, "It's all about the money" was looping in her head like some sort of '80s dance mix. The music came to a halt when the door opened and one of the most handsome military cuts in a dress shirt and tie walked out to shake her hand.

Jocelyn, who was holding her driver's license, birth certificate and passport stood up to greet him. All smiles, she said, "I brought everything I need. I'll even do the fingerprints if you want." She held up her hand and wiggled her fingers.

"That's probably not necessary right now. Why don't you tell me what brings you here."

Jocelyn got the distinct impression that this Secret Service guy was speaking to her like a psychologist, and she took her enthusiasm level down a notch.

"The chairman of the Republican party says that the Secret Service needs to do three levels of a security clearance..."

A few good minutes of confusion ping ponged around the waiting area until Jocelyn took the questionnaire out of her bag to show him.

"Well, this doesn't look too professional. Who gave this to you again?"

By the time Jocelyn and Mr. Handsome Secret Service Guy finally parted ways, it had been explained to her that the only people who would be getting background checks would be the vendors driving trucks into and out of the convention center. He said that he would double check with the Tampa office to confirm that, but the only time they ever needed to do any sort of wholesale sweep was on a short suspense visit of the President.

"And we probably wouldn't ask you for your social security number. A driver's license maybe. I don't think we've ever asked for a social security number. We have other ways of checking you out that are more effective for our needs."

When she got home she did a Google search for 'RNC, Republicans, social security number' and instantly found an article published by the *New York Sun* from October 1, 2006.

Oh, no way.

CHAPTER TWENTY-FIVE

THE FOLLOWING FRIDAY EVENING, Jocelyn arrived at the Ivy League Alumni Club, a stately Colonial Georgian brick house in the historic section of Providence, across the street from the Central Intelligence Agency's branch office. Tasteful flower arrangements adorned the foyer and hallways. Butlers took coats and offered drinks. The vibe of the place reminded Jocelyn very much of Drumthwaket, the governor's mansion in New Jersey, where she had accidentally found herself years ago, but this was nowhere near as spacious. Possibly as pretentious, though.

"Well, congratulations *delegates!* I am very happy to see you all here tonight," the chairman of the state GOP said in his master of ceremonies voice.

Everyone found a seat at one of the little cocktail tables that had been elegantly set with white linen, silver, and a fragrant bud vase arrangement of white freesia. It appeared that all the former Republican governors and mayors of the state had been elected as delegates for presidential candidate Kitt Rooney. This was not surprising as they all had name recognition and were obviously active within the party. What was surprising to Jocelyn was that all their wives had run for the position of delegate, too, and had also won the honor of being a delegate for Kitt Rooney. It was these women who, like a brood of chicks, came over and started pecking at her about what type of hat she was going to wear.

"Hat? We have to wear hats?"

"Oh, see, she doesn't know. She's never been to one before!" exclaimed a well-manicured woman who obviously had a plastic surgeon at her disposal.

"Honey, it's a tradition," another woman helpfully added.

"Everyone wears a hat that represents their state. Like, the Texas delegation always comes wearing cowboy hats."

"So men wear hats, too?"

"I guess they could if they wanted to..."

Jocelyn nodded, feigning a high level of interest.

"And then you decorate it. Just go wild. Make it your own."

"I've been working on mine already," an elderly woman with fleshy, 'forever fuchsia' lips nearly barked. "I've put silk flowers all around the crown, and there are teabags hanging from the brim."

"Oh, how clever!"

"Okay! Okay! Ladies, the meeting is about to start. Please have a seat. We have a lot of important business to discuss before we head to Tampa," the master of ceremonies announced again.

Darn straight, we have business to discuss.

Jocelyn didn't want to embarrass the state chair. He was a nice enough guy. He came to her book club fairly regularly, but he was wrong, and she wasn't going to include her social security number. She had already told the other RP delegates not to do it either.

"Okay, everybody! So the first order of business pertains to our state pin! What's it gonna look like?" the state chair dramatically announced. The woman who had been all excited about hats mentioned that she could order the pins from a company she dealt with. Then everyone discussed what should be featured on the pin. The state bird? A boat?

"What are we talking about?" Jocelyn whispered to the man at the next table.

"Oh, for the convention, each state has pins made up. Everyone buys a bunch, and when you go to another state's cocktail party, you trade a pin from our state for a pin from their state. That way, by time you leave the convention, you have a lapel full of different pins."

Jocelyn was becoming more and more disenchanted with

this whole thing. Here she was, dressed for success, all ready to get to work putting the country back on track, and everyone was sitting around in the lap of luxury sipping wine, discussing funny hats and trading pins. Plus, she was getting anxious about this social security thing. She was bracing herself for that confrontation.

Just then, a good-looking, dark-haired young man who appeared as if he had just left work at a car wash came into the room. Everyone turned to look at him. His attire was obviously out of place, not to mention his Puerto Rican lineage, considering every single person at this party was whiter than white. A butler rushed in and hurriedly offered him a jacket, which he refused.

"Did I miss anything?"

"No, no, Ricardo," the chairman smiled. "Please have a seat. We've been discussing this year's pin. Now that you're here, we might as well talk about committee positions."

Ricardo was an RP delegate and a student at the community college. He hadn't been involved in the election four years ago because he had been too young to vote, but he had been a fan of Ray Pierce because of all the YouTube clips and podcasts since then. So Jocelyn didn't know him very well at all. He had gotten a ton of votes during the election, most likely because he had a ton of 'friends' on Facebook and because of his sprawling extended family. He was the very embodiment of 'viral' marketing.

When Ricardo had seated himself and the discussion turned to the vacant committee positions, Jocelyn was surprised that no one in the room seemed at all interested in being on a committee. There were quite a few committees up for grabs. Each state committee needed one female and one male representative. Jocelyn had volunteered for Platform Committee but was informed that she was the wrong sex.

"We really need you guys to step up!" the chairman coaxed.

Ricardo stood up, raised his hand, and said, "I'll go." He

ended up on the Platform Committee because no one wanted to go to that. This committee was a real commitment because it met for an entire week before the actual convention, meaning that more money was needed for lodging. Ricardo whispered to Jocelyn that he wouldn't be able to afford it. Jocelyn whispered back that they would do an online fundraiser to get him there. They'd figure it out. Platform was an important committee. It was basically a steering committee that designed what the party would stand for, at least until the next election. It was a way to get Ray Pierce's ideas embedded into the very fabric of the Republican party.

The chairman and his wife ended up on a bunch of committees because no one else seemed able to get to Tampa early for the meetings. "That's fine. Gives me a chance to network," the chairman said.

Finally, the State GOP meeting's business was over, and the chair and his wife were getting ready to leave. Jocelyn purposefully sauntered over to him and shook his hand, thanking him for such an exquisite meeting place. She also let him know that she was very excited to attend the RNC as she produced the delegate questionnaire and handed it to him.

"Oh, thank you, Jocelyn. Now I can get those guys off my back."

"I didn't fill out the social security number, and you'll notice a bunch of other Ray Pierce people didn't do it, either." His hand instantly reached down into his tote bag and grabbed for the stack of questionnaires. He started flipping through them to confirm what she had just said. "I'm pretty sure you are just following orders, but I went to Social Security, and I went to the Secret Service and..."

"You did? Secret Service? How far away was that?"

Jocelyn pointed out the window. "The court house building."

The chairman's wife was instantly involved, and in what sounded like a panic said, "Everyone *must* provide a social security number or they are *not* going to be allowed entry."

"No. That's not the case at all. I checked it out and..." She noticed that the chairman had wandered away and was munching on the picked over bits of cheese at the appetizer table.

"The RNC is a private club! If you don't follow their directions and they don't want to let you in, they don't have to!" The chairman's wife was shaking as she said it.

"That may be true, but what is going on right now may very easily be construed as harassment of duly elected delegates." Jocelyn was cool because she knew she was right. She also knew other states across the country were having one hell of a time with hardcore RP delegate harassment. Even violence was involved. A huge, sweeping lawsuit was being crafted as they spoke against the merger of the Rooney campaign and the RNC and its treatment of Raymond Pierce delegates.

The chairman wandered back when he heard Jocelyn say, "Look, I didn't want to bring it up during the meeting. I didn't want to embarrass your husband in front of..."

The chairman put his hand on his wife's shoulder and somehow the whole thing quietly ended with him saying, "I'll see you in Tampa, Jocelyn."

CHAPTER TWENTY-SIX

ETHAN HAD BEEN RIGHT. Things had calmed down considerably since she told Jerry that he had to leave. It was weird when they said goodbye because it was like they were breaking up or something. She had dropped Jerry at the train station, and he had tried to hug her in the car. It was almost as uncomfortable and unexpectedly disastrous as trying to properly handle a gun while twisted about in the driver's seat in a dark library parking lot.

It was a good three minutes of all sorts of unnecessary drama. He sounded like he was going to say something, but then he didn't. Then it seemed like he was going to try to kiss her, but then he didn't. When they finally did hug, it was prefaced by an awkward weaving and bobbing of their heads as they established a left- or right-sided approach to the embrace. When they did fully engage in the much anticipated climatic hug, Jocelyn ended up exclaiming, "Ouch!" because it felt like he was breaking her rib.

Flooding her with apologies, he instantly let go of her and touched her hand before he hopped out of the car. But it wasn't over. He opened the door back up, leaned in and passed her a folded piece of paper. It was tucked into itself like how she used to fold notes in Junior High School.

"Tear it up. Or burn it. Okay?"

She nodded. She could have sworn he had tears in his eyes. After he slammed the car door shut, put on his sunglasses and ran into the station, Jocelyn opened the note. All it said, in his own handwriting, was: I love wingdings.

"Well, gee, thanks, Jerry! That's it?" she said while flipping the paper over to see if anything else was written on it.

She burned it later that night. She had to admit that she did find the burning of his note somehow meaningful, but she hadn't seen or heard from Jerry since she had watched him run into the station. She imagined that he was back to being a fully-fledged, wingding lovin' ghost.

Meanwhile, Ethan was paying his child support and taking the kids regularly for dinners and overnights. She really couldn't ask for anything more, but she did. She asked him to install some cameras around the cabin, nothing major. Maybe some of those motion-activated cameras that she had found so irritating in the past. Or maybe a webcam. You know, just in case. She wasn't asking for a full house alarm system or anything like that. He declined.

"You're gonna be fine, Joss. Don't worry. Okay?"

She was a little miffed that he wouldn't do it now that she was actually asking him directly for something that he himself used to be a big proponent of. She needed something for added security, didn't she? She'd pay for everything. He just sort of shrugged and said, "Just live life, Joss."

"Easy for you to say, Ethan! You don't have perverted old congressmen calling you or cars blowing up. And what about that Starbucks employee who got shot by the dumpster?"

He kind of raised his eyebrows and smirked. He ended up taking her to the range a few times to show her how to use that Berretta more effectively, and while all the cacophony of the range hammered on, she recognized that he was beginning to show the familiar signs of his biennial swing to being in love with her again. Or at least it seemed that way. Although she was very, very leery, it was nice to be showered with gifts. It almost made her forget about the times when he was clearly anti-Jocelyn and would confuse the hell out of her with his lies about lies.

Ethan took back the StreetSweeper and gave her a brand new, more traditional-looking shotgun for home security purposes. Apparently, the StreetSweeper was near and dear to his heart. “I got this baby in Serbia,” he said, as a twisted type of sentimental smile crept across his features.

She only half-believed him but figured it was probably true. Naturally, Jocelyn didn’t think to ask how he had gotten the thing back into this country; and of course, she was willfully ignorant of any licensing or permits needed on her part for the Beretta or the shotgun.

Things, compared to the recent Jerry chaos, seemed surprisingly normal. She had adopted Ethan’s thinking that everything weird that she had experienced was because of Jerry. At least now the day was organized into a pattern she recognized, however dysfunctional it was. She had become almost professional at suppressing enormous amounts of anxiety about being murdered. Jocelyn’s technique: focus on mundane details. Straightening up the house (dusting excluded, of course) while whistling the same children’s song about a ladybug over and over became downright clinical.

With the RNC coming up quickly, and because of those ladies at the GOP meeting, she had begun to fret about what she was going to wear. Especially irritating was that stupid hat thing.

“Like, I got elected to march around in a funny hat,” she griped to Ethan over a chicken chimichanga. Ethan had taken her out to lunch at the local Tex-Mex joint. The kids were with her mother. “If I have to wear a hat, I want a really dramatic, over the top, beautiful hat.” She swirled her arm above her head for added drama.

He smirked. “Knock yourself out, Joss,” he said as he squeezed the lime into his Corona. “As I’ve mentioned countless times now,” he commented as he popped the rind into the bottle, “it’s just a game. Nothing ever changes because of an election. If it did, they’d probably make the whole process illegal.”

This time (probably because they were out in public) instead of barking his anarchistic philosophy at her, he was more mild-mannered about it, which encouraged her to think out loud. She appreciated this. At least he listened to her. At this point, with Jocelyn's now encyclopedic knowledge of all things miserable and apocalyptic, a lot of people didn't care to speak with her. Even her mother had told her to stop sending emails because she couldn't handle the depressing topics Jocelyn was bringing up in conversation.

So, Jocelyn was happy to have someone with whom to at least be out in public. Someone who knew what the heck she was even talking about, and someone who made her feel safe. She and Ethan batted around some ideas about what she should wear to the convention to make a statement. With his help, she came up with a five day plan for her wardrobe. The fifth day would be the day she would wear the hat. By the time lunch was over, she felt as if she owed him something for taking time out of his busy schedule to be with her and for the $4.99 chimichanga.

The two of them left the little restaurant with its bright colors and mariachi music and headed to the parking lot.

"Hey, thanks for lunch," she smiled.

"Don't mention it."

"No. Seriously, this meant a lot to me." She looked at her shoes and said, "It was nice to be out of the house and talking with an adult."

Jocelyn heard him start laughing, but then he stopped. He edged closer to her and lightly touched her cheek. She looked up and the two made eye contact. For whatever crazy reason, they ended up in his truck and lost all track of time. When she finally said goodbye and hopped out, she noticed that Ethan's windows were thoroughly steamed up. Although her heart was light from the experience, she could feel herself blushing as she headed back to her mommy-mobile.

CHAPTER TWENTY-SEVEN

THE NEXT DAY, Ethan sent her a gigantic flower arrangement littered with white roses, casa blanca lilies, and white dendrobium orchids. It was a veritable bridal bouquet thanking her for enjoying *his* chimichanga.

She knew that most women would be thrilled with this display, but she wasn't happy. She was upset with herself for doing what she did in the Tex-Mex parking lot at lunch. She felt like an alcoholic who had just fallen off the wagon. This guy, Ethan, was bad medicine. She knew it, but why did she have to do *that*? If she had still been trotting off to her counselor's office once a week, the pesky topic that religiously kept popping up like a spastic hedgehog—self-esteem—would have been discussed. Again.

That night, she decided to quit beating herself up about it and just look for the imaginary hat she was lusting after. It needed to be classy, not like something your grandma wears to church. Something dramatic and... What was it that she was trying to express with this hat anyway, she wondered.

She wasn't stupid. She recognized the obviousness of Ray Pierce's likelihood of losing. Anyone who had lived through the election four years ago knew this was going to be an absolute nightmare, even though they had the required amount of states and could nominate RP from the floor. But the scene with the Iowa Caucus had pretty much set the tone for what was to come at the convention.

Ray Pierce won the caucus. The DailyPierce website had been aflutter with live reports from on the ground. This was exactly as his supporters had anticipated because this is what they had worked for since last election. Iowa was an important caucus because it was the earliest, and winning it was the equivalent of a giant television commercial airing everywhere. Party members have the tendency to follow the leader, and the winner of Iowa influenced a lot of votes in other states.

However, that night, all of the news outlets reported that Kitt Rooney had won Iowa by eight votes. *What? Seriously? No way...* Then two weeks later, after some controversy, unbelievably, these same news outlets ran the story that yet another candidate had actually won Iowa.

Eventually, after a recount, it was discovered that eight full precincts' worth of votes had gone missing. By time the general television consuming public, which everyone knows has the attention span of a fruit fly, was completely fatigued with the topic of the Iowa Caucus and had moved on to another controversy de jour, it was quietly revealed that Ray Pierce had somehow won Iowa. The positive public relations impact had been lost. The messaging that RP was unelectable was in full force. Operation 'Follow the Leader' was in effect, and there was nothing anyone could do about it. The DailyPeirce website was alive with supporters from all over the country complaining to each other and trying to figure out the best way to explain how this was even possible to their family members who were thoroughly convinced that the major news channels couldn't possibly be lying to them.

Maine had a similar situation. Now, to those familiar with the latitude and longitude of the state of Maine, it should come as no surprise that it might snow in February. Heck, Maine residents use snowmobiles to go to the grocery store. Amazingly, some of the key Ray Pierce precincts were rescheduling their caucus because of a *possible* snowstorm, which never occurred. It was reported far and wide that Kitt Rooney had won that state, but just like Iowa, RP actually won the Maine delegates—all of them. Of course, the news outlets and their devoted audiences congratulated Kitt Rooney on how much more electable he was compared to any of the other candidates. This sort of stuff was happening all over the place and at a dizzying pace.

All this election stuff was just irritating. Irritating because she was feeling the divide. Not just between the world view of the Democrats and Republicans, which was always heated, and not just within the Republican party itself, but between the television watchers and the Internet users. This technological divide, which she had picked up on during the last presidential election, was now being obviously and rigorously exploited and was causing a fissure within her own extended family. It was making communication about real issues almost impossible. Like some sort of Mandelbrot Fractal oil spill, that whole 'divide and conquer' thing had begun to take on tangible form.

She felt as if the only legitimate skill she had to counter this assault, her Conglomerate marketing and PR experience, was now serving solely to piss her off. Knowing and watching how obscene amounts of money were directing the public's attention and actions was becoming a filthy, daily frustration. She knew people could only make decisions based upon what they were exposed to. She also knew that what they were exposed to on TV, or even on the radio, was exclusively about increasing shareholder value. It was that simple. 'The People' were being systematically manipulated on a huge scale.

With all this on her mind, she clicked around the selection of glamorous hats and thought especially about what Ethan had been saying—that it was all about money. *Is money even the right word for all this? Or is something else going on here?*

She hatched a plan. One she thought that even Ethan would support. She was convinced the plan made sense and would work, given what she was officially reduced to. I mean, in what better way could one woman, a certifiably bankrupt floral designer who exchanged oral sex for a chimichanga, fight back against such a monster? Her plan, she concluded, was most elegant.

CHAPTER TWENTY-EIGHT

The same day
International Plaza and Bay Street
Tampa, Florida

MIŠEL GUJIC, NOW ASSUMING the name Michelle Jones, crossed her arms over her chest and sucked on her cheek as she waited for Heartbreaker to finish trying on the tall, black leather, high-heel boot. The two of them had already been to Louis Vuitton, and Michelle was getting pissed. She hadn't trotted all the way here to Nordstrom just to watch this woman try on expensive footwear.

"Those boots are exactly like the ones you just tried on," Michelle sniffed as she adjusted her sensible Timex watch. Her hair was done up in a Dorothy Hamill cut, and her glasses were something out of the same era, pinkish plastic with rather large rims. She looked every bit the part of a Weather Channel disgruntled employee. That was because she was living it. She landed the job, no problem, during one of the company's layoff blitzkriegs. She was simply dealing with faxes, teletype, emails, and RSS feeds. That's all she did, all day—every day. Boring. So when she got the message to meet up with Heartbreaker, even though she hated the woman, she was excited to get back into the game.

"No. These boots come with little buckle. See?" Heartbreaker said, standing up to admire the positive attributes of the little buckle in the mirror as she shifted the position of her feet. Unlike Michelle, Heartbreaker was adorned in the latest Joseph Altuzarra's collection. Michelle found it to be an ugly a blend of nautical-military-Gypsy-influences and had told her as much when they first met.

Exasperated, Michelle said, “Kuja, can we get this over with? I’ve only got so much time for my lunch break.” Heartbreaker did not seem at all phased to be called a ‘bitch’ in Bosnian and asked the salesperson, in what Mišel perceived as an overtly passive/aggressive smack in the face, if she might try on the same boots in brown.

“I love this boot,” Heartbreaker gushed. “Is boot I wear in Italy. That was good job,” she smiled as she said it.

“Great. That’s wonderful. Look, I did up a simple, quick fix. Do you want it or not?”

Heartbreaker glanced at Michelle in the mirror and said simply, “I do not need.”

“Well, fine. Maybe *you* should just eat this then,” she sneered as she jammed a small, very cold thing about the size of a PopTart, wrapped in aluminum foil, into Heartbreaker’s purse.

Heartbreaker spun around on her buckled heels when she saw Michelle touching her purse and was ready to pounce just as the salesperson appeared with the brown boots. She ignored the salesperson and strode directly to stand face to face with Michelle, who did not seem at all bothered. “I froze it. If it’s not completely thawed out by now, it should be good for a long time. Jebi se, and have good day.” She adjusted the strap of her purse, threw one more look of pure unadulterated hatred at Heartbreaker, and headed for the exit.

CHAPTER TWENTY-NINE

Weeks later
The Republican National Convention
Tampa, Florida

JOCELYN HAD ARRIVED SUNDAY just in time to make Ray Pierce's pre-convention rally at the Sun Dome. Because she was a delegate, she got a VIP pass for the private party in the luxury box. She even helped sneak in the *Providence Journal* reporter, who didn't have a VIP pass. There had been over five thousand people there, but naturally, the local Tampa newspaper was quoted as saying only five hundred showed up. Of course, the five hundred number made sense because of the impending hurricane that had been hyped in the national media for the past three days.

Jocelyn knew hurricanes were to Florida what snowstorms were to Maine, and true to form, there was no hurricane on Monday. Rainy and blustery for sure, but the hurricane wasn't even supposed to hit Florida until Wednesday, if it hit Florida at all. The RNC was suspended because of it anyway. Of course, Ray Pierce was supposed to speak on Monday—the day he could have been nominated from the convention floor because he had the majority of delegates in five states. Those were the rules.

Jocelyn and a bunch of RP delegates had decided to brave the so-called hurricane and show up at the convention hall anyway despite the RNC's memo to just luxuriate at the hotel or go shopping (during a hurricane, no less). If the party chairman was brave enough to weather the storm and strike the gavel calling off the meeting, then so were they, to witness it. *Robert's Rules of Order* and all that.

At this point, she had gone through the metal detectors and the cursory credential checks. She entered, with almost the same reverence as she would a cathedral, into the enormous space that teams of union workers had prepared especially for them. The place was just about deserted except for the unionized audio visual crew in the control box and the full security detail.

She'd been to trade shows and sporting events, so she knew the layout. A modern day Colosseum-for-hire. Jumbotron and sound system dangled from the center of the ceiling. Wall-to-wall, blue-with-stars specialty carpet covered the vast expanse of the floor. The whole floor of the convention hall had been set up with hundreds of black folding chairs, and fifty state names had been hoisted up on poles throughout the space indicating everyone's proper position when the big party started.

Eight-foot-tall white letters hung on two PrismaColor-matched blue walls, spelling out the marketing slogans of the party. Namely, that the Republicans had built the nation and how they could do a better job than the current president. Naturally, those messages had been installed by union workers as well.

Jocelyn's inner brand manager immediately noticed the similarity to the blue sign she and the RP folks back home had painted and hung off the parking garage. She knew *they* knew, as well. The RNC had used the same Palatino font that Jocelyn's friends had painstakingly traced and enlarged from the Pierce campaign material. *Tricky bastards.*

Most people wouldn't pick up on the subtleties, but to her, this was huge. The RNC must have known that the Ray Pierce campaign would not—or could not—complain as the RNC attempted to steal a powerful cache of emotions and random soundbite memories associated with RP. This was the very essence of branding. She remembered how she had been forced to redo two sets of five binders' worth of finished proposals because she had used the wrong font. This branding thing was serious business. Imagine seeing something like the word 'Coca-Cola' or 'Microsoft' in a different typeface? Oh, the horror!

She had experienced the same sick feeling when she had seen the headlines splashed all over the place announcing: ROONEY PICKS PIERCE! Rooney had not picked Raymond Pierce as his vice-presidential running mate as the headline might have people infer by the use of Kitt Rooney's last name. No. He had picked Pierce Roland. A guy who conveniently also had two first names *and* the same initials to further confuse the general population when Team Rooney—which was now its own legal entity, comprising RNC lawyers and some select Rooney Campaign staff—started firing off the 'Pierce is an economic genius!' press releases.

Dressed in her Day One outfit, a gray, tastefully form-fitting, above the knee, starburst shutter dress and a pair of sensible heels, she wandered over to the vertical placard announcing where her state's delegates were supposed to sit and sat down in one of the folding chairs. She was studying the elaborate set design, the multiple layers of large-format video screens accented with Vegas-style colorful lighting. She wondered how the fabrication costs compared to that thing she had done up for the AUSA show for General Walton back during her Conglomerate days. *I can't even imagine! This is just... just so over the top. And what a ridiculously lame set design.*

There were about one hundred Ray Pierce delegates ambling around the labyrinth of folding chairs when a woman she had never met before sat down next to her. The petite woman, twenty-something-ish, was wearing a red, full-length halter top dress. Her luxurious long black hair ran down her almond-skinned back, and most obviously, she was topped off with a straw cowboy hat with an American flag bandana wrapped around the crown. They smiled at each other.

"Nice hat. I see you got the memo," Jocelyn attempted to

joke. The woman looked confused but smiled. They sat for a few more moments in silence as the rest of the empty room mulled around. Jocelyn noticed the lady's shoes. *Very cool.* Jocelyn's best guess was that they looked like some sort of John Fluevog number. "I like your shoes."

The woman smiled again. "Would you like to try?" the woman asked. She had some sort of foreign accent that Jocelyn couldn't place. Her features looked as if maybe she was the product of an Italian and Middle Eastern marriage. The woman in red blinked and smiled as she slipped her foot out of the shoe. *Oh, how odd?* Jocelyn had not been expecting the woman to actually let her try on the footwear.

Noticing the shoe size listed as US 8, Jocelyn politely chuckled, "Oh, I'd never fit in that." The woman took it back and replaced it on her foot.

Jocelyn fought the urge to kick this person out of the clearly marked state delegation area. She didn't know why she was getting so territorial. The entire conference center was pretty much empty. If everything hadn't been so darn sparkly new, she would not have been surprised to see a tumbleweed roll by. It was that deserted. "I don't think I've ever met you before. I'm Jocelyn. Jocelyn McLaren. But on the DailyPierce, I'm LadyLiberty70," she said with a friendly smile.

Just then, before the introductions could be made properly, the Jumbotron above them flickered to life and some stock music started blaring from the sound system. A pre-recorded sportscaster's voice let everyone know that he was pleased to announce that the National Chairman would be convening this year's RNC in a few moments.

Less than thirty seconds went by. The National Chair entered stage right, and the logo for the Republican National Convention scrolled slowly through the elaborate set of oversized video monitors behind him. He welcomed everyone to the convention and officially started the meeting. Then, in the next sentence, he officially adjourned the meeting until further notice, banged the gavel down, and walked off the stage. There was some mumbling amongst the audience as to what that technically meant as per *Robert's Rules of Order,* and then the video screens snapped to life.

It was a good one minute of presidential candidate Kitt Rooney delivering his "I believe in America that Americans believe live in America" speech with images of him holding children and shaking hands. This was quickly montaged with sparks flying from some automobile production line, and another screen featured wheat and corn rustling in the breeze. A tractor was in there, too, at one point.

All the screens on stage were projecting different disjointed narratives of American productivity. It finally concluded with Rooney looking very approachable in a white oxford, top button unbuttoned, sleeves rolled up, humbly pleased to take on the challenge of fixing this great nation as he looked out beyond the camera into the optimistic future.

The room went wild! Crowd cheering! Clapping! Hoots and hollers! The whole shebang. Jocelyn looked at the woman next to her and then around the room. She was confused. Who was cheering? There was practically no one there. Jocelyn had assumed that everyone in attendance was a Ray Pierce fan. Upon closer inspection, she confirmed that assumption. It *was* a room full of RP people. The cheering had been pre-recorded. Eventually, all the screens went back to scrolling the convention's logo, and then finally to black. Illumination would come soon enough.

After the pre-recorded Rooney speech finished and the screens had finally been shut off, it was obvious to those in attendance that there was nothing left to do there except tack some Ray Pierce signs on and around the eight-foot lettering on the wall. Jocelyn didn't participate in that. Although she found it rather childish, she did appreciate the spectacle of it from her folding chair. She leaned over with a smirk and asked the woman in the red dress where she was from. Thinking that she'd say some multicultural locale like New

York City, she was surprised to hear the woman's response.

"Serbia."

"Hmmm. Then how come you're here?" Jocelyn asked, eying the credentials hanging around the woman's neck. "Don't you need to be an American to be elected as a delegate?"

"Oh, I'm American now. I have citizenship."

"Congratulations," Jocelyn said, smiling. "That's a big deal."

"It was the happiest day of my life."

"I can imagine."

"No. No, you can't. I used to pray to the heavenly father and ask him why. Why, dear papa, is it that the Americans are doing this to us? I was so scared. I cried and cried to my papa. And when I was done crying, I would go mad. The bombs would go boom boom all night. Boom boom! My sweet papa would cradle me and say, 'Go with the Americans. Be with them. They will bring you bring freedom.'"

At this point, Jocelyn was having a hard time discerning if the woman was talking about the heavenly father or her birth father. It didn't matter. She was intense, and Jocelyn didn't want to stop her mid-flow to ask for clarification. The woman took Jocelyn's hands and held them in each of hers. Jocelyn got the distinct impression that the woman was going to start praying or something.

"You have the eyes of an angel. Eyes like the ocean—blue. You see. You see things others have not..."

Okay, this was getting weird. This woman was smiling like she was experiencing some sort of beatific vision and looking so deeply and intensely into Jocelyn's eyes that the hairs on Jocelyn's arms and the back of her neck started to stand on up edge. Jocelyn wasn't sure exactly how to tactfully extract her hands from this woman's grasp. Then again, she wasn't sure if she really wanted to if, in fact, the woman was in mid-prayer or teetering between the here and now and some sort of spiritual nether world.

The two stayed locked in each other's gaze for what seemed a timeless and soundless lifetime. If Jocelyn had been actually listening to this woman speak and not partially hypnotized, she would have only heard the tale. What was happening now was not auditory. Jocelyn was feeling it. It was as if the woman was transferring all of the emotions and sensations of being a child prostitute directly to Jocelyn's limbic system.

Still holding hands with the Lady-in-Red in the middle of the deserted convention center, Jocelyn learned how this woman's oldest sister had been mangled and left for dead while working the streets. After that, it had been a blessing to be included in ex-general Claude Vaughn's stable. At the tender age of eleven, she worked with her fourteen-year-old sister, and they had excellent protection because of this ex-general. He was very well-respected, and no one wanted to get on his bad side. They had been trained to call all the Johns 'Colonel' and learned how working together would make things safer. The Americans who purchased their services typically paid well; only rarely did a colonel cut or hurt one of them because if he did, he would not be allowed back. Sometimes, her mother even got a tip for cooking the colonel breakfast. The scene being painted in Jocelyn's mind was an odd mix of Norman Rockwell meets Pablo Picasso's *Guernica*.

As Jocelyn struggled to cognitively untangle and make sense of it all, the convention center's lights flickered on and off, and the sports announcer's pre-recorded voice blasted out that the convention hall would be shutting down in fifteen minutes. Jocelyn and the woman let go of each other's hands, and Jocelyn, because she needed to look anywhere else other than at the woman's eyes, noticed a small tattoo on the woman's right wrist. It was of a heart. A heart torn into two pieces.

"I'm sorry, I never caught your name," Jocelyn, still reeling from the exchange, said as she gathered up her pocketbook.

“Oh, it’s Stojanka, but most call me Heartbreaker.”

CHAPTER THIRTY

RNC Day Two

"HEY, I WATCHED IT YESTERDAY and the crowd was really diggin' Rooney."

"No. No, the crowd wasn't diggin' Rooney"

"What do you mean? I saw it on TV."

Ethan had called her early that morning to check in on her and let her know that the kids were fine and missing her. Jocelyn gave him the rundown of the previous day's events. She knew he could really care less, but he did seem somewhat interested in hearing about the hurricane that wasn't and the woman who had been sitting next to her.

"It was really nuts, Ethan..."

Jocelyn didn't tell Ethan the whole story about Heartbreaker because it was too hard to explain without sounding like a complete lunatic, and because during the night, she had developed a nagging suspicion about Ethan and this woman. The only other times she recalled hearing the name Heartbreaker were in a Led Zeppelin song and in that weird text that Ethan had sent her after she had found that size eight stiletto shoe in their yard.

It was crazy, she knew, but she figured it was probably best to bury that theory with her other suppressed fears of getting tortured with a butterfly pin or her kids getting kidnapped. So she just let him know that this woman, Stojanka, and she had bonded over some cool shoes and that she had to get off the phone.

Anyway, today was the first official day of the convention, since yesterday had been cancelled. She wore her

Day Two outfit, a fawn-colored Calvin Klein fitted sheath dress. She had selected it because of the black color block square positioned off center on her chest. It reminded her of a black flag. After yesterday's 'hurricane' and Rooney video presentation, she thought it appropriate.

The delegates convened for breakfast and listened as to why Carol Hennesy, the state's female RNC member, explained why it decided to change everyone's stance on the Party Rules during a late-night emergency meeting. As of yesterday, Jocelyn's state supported something called the Minority Report, a document crafted by a gentleman from Virginia who opposed changing the party's rules on such short notice.

"I mean, they've had four years to suggest this, and they waited until *now*?" one of the older men who had been to something like six of these conventions, rudely interrupted.

"These rule changes don't really affect us, Charlie," Carol said, adjusting her microphone to face the irritated man. "We are a Primary state. The rule changes would mostly impact caucus states by requiring delegate allocation be bound to that state's straw-poll results. The final delegate count for a candidate would not be connected to the actual delegates that the caucus voted for."

"But there were more changes, too!" Charlie yelled. He was now standing and pointing at Carol as he passionately spoke. Everyone else seemed like they were trying to politely ignore him, like he was a crazy drunk uncle or something. Jocelyn found this exchange interesting because she knew the states in which Pierce had done well were the ones affected. "Carol! That one change in particular could make it virtually impossible for a movement candidate to become the nominee!"

"Charlie, you're a Rooney delegate. I don't know why you are so upset."

"Do you remember *why* you signed the Minority Report in the first place? It's because Rhode Island fully supports the

Minority Report and you... you just took it upon yourself to—"

"Well, Charlie, I agree with your first statement. They've had ample time to vet this. I didn't like how Rooney's lawyer wanted to do this on the fly. They could have proposed this three years ago. Or they could wait until the next round of Rules Committee meetings. I signed the first Minority Report because of that. I just didn't think it appropriate."

"So what made you change your mind in the middle of the night and sign the compromise to accept the changes?" Charlie wanted to know.

"Well, the lawyers changed some of the grammar, and as most of you know, I am an English teacher, and I appreciate attention to grammar. I think it's important, especially at this point during the convention, to be perceived as a united front against the sitting president."

Everyone made a weak effort to clap between eating their poor excuse of a pancake and greasy sausage. Charlie was still upset, though, and was mumbling in a voice loud enough for everyone to hear, "Why are they changing the rules now? This is crazy. These lawyers can't just walk in here and do this. This isn't how *my* party works." Jocelyn noticed him tossing a furtive look at the RNC woman as he continued, "And she went along with it? I wonder if they paid her?"

Then, after everyone had gotten seconds at the buffet, some female governor from another state came in to talk about how the Republicans were really trying to focus on the "women's vote."

Jocelyn listened politely as she munched on her cheese Danish and sipped her decaffeinated coffee. The combo of the early morning meeting, coffee, and cheese Danish must have tripped some sort of memory center in her brain. It started a rousing round of 'I'm awake and alive and I feel great!' inside her head. The flashback to her "executive training for women seminar" was most likely induced by sheer physical exhaustion. She and a bunch of RP people she had never met before (and who kept referring to her by her DailyPierce moniker, LadyLiberty) had been up pretty much the whole night stuffing photocopies under hotel room doors.

Vote NO! on the rules change!
Support the Minority Report!
Save the party! Save the Republic!

Even as she was hunched over slipping the notes under the doors of the sleeping delegates' rooms, she was getting pissed. She wanted to save the country, not the party, and here she was losing sleep about party rules. This was ridiculous.

Anyhow, she was tired.

After they all listened to that governor talk about the importance of women, they filed out to the front entrance of the hotel and waited for the bus that would take them to the convention center. Everyone was dressed to the hilt and feeling very important. Finally, twenty minutes late, a large charter bus arrived, and like good schoolchildren, everyone jockeyed for position to get onto the thing.

The bus was about half-full, and Jocelyn was still waiting her turn when she noticed people getting off the bus they had just gotten on. Confusion swept across the waiting delegates until everyone was made aware that the charter bus they were all staring at was for some sort of Oyster Fest. It wasn't going anywhere near the convention center. So everyone stood around or went to the bar for the next forty-five minutes and waited for the right bus.

It was during this waiting period that Jocelyn found out that the delegates from the state of Virginia and the gentleman who had crafted that Minority Report were waiting to get on the same bus. They were freaking out because the Rules Committee meeting was supposed to be happening soon, and no one could get a taxi.

"Why did they have to put us in a hotel so far away from

the convention?! This is insane." The people still standing outside waiting for the bus mumbled in agreement, and Jocelyn fought back a tired giggle. A wife/delegate eyed her disapprovingly, so Jocelyn started talking to the doorman to kill time.

Finally, a charter bus pulled up. Everyone, looking a little worse for wear, attempted the second take of muscling their way onto the bus. As soon as the bus was full of people, folks started getting off. Apparently, this bus was for delegates only. Alternate delegates and spouses and even the press had to go on a different bus.

"Well, where the hell is *that* bus?"

"Right down the street."

Rest assured, the Alternate Delegate/Spouse bus was not right down the street. Even if it had been, they would probably need another bus, too, because they would be over the seating capacity limit with the inclusion of the Virginia delegation's spouses.

"So tell me again about what a great job Rooney did organizing those Olympics? This sucks!"

The folks left on the sidewalk were getting really annoyed as the delegate bus, which had made room for an armed female parole officer (you know, for protection), pulled out onto the main road.

Finally! Everyone was breathing a sigh of relief, but that relief would be quickly replaced by full-on sweaty-palmed panic. The traffic was abysmal getting into Tampa. Stop. Go. Stop. Go. People were becoming obsessed with looking at their watches and counting down how many minutes they had left to get themselves to the Rules Committee meeting.

If those new rules passed, the general rules of the party could be changed on a whim by the Republican National Committee at any time. *If* those new rules passed, Ray Pierce would not be able to be nominated from the floor. This was an incredible move on the part of Rooney's lawyer who, incidentally, would be officially working for the White House within a year.

Finally, after the driver, apparently not familiar with the area, snaked into and out of the city multiple times and the parole officer jumped out to move one of the Jersey barriers, they reached the "Green Zone," the blocked-off, secure part of town surrounding the convention center. However, by moving the Jersey barrier and following the formerly blocked-off road, the bus found itself driving at a snail's pace as part of some sort of small protest.

Riot-geared police lined the streets in shoulder-to-shoulder formation. Calvary police were assembled at the street corners, and the latest and greatest in urban warfare, a black street tank, sat proudly for its photo op in front of the court house. All the clock watching delegates on the bus sat in frustration as the 'Food Not Bombs' sign slowly led the way.

"That's fucking it! I can see the fucking convention center right fucking there!" That's when Jocelyn started losing it. She just couldn't stop laughing. It was the worst time to start laughing because the guy who was swearing his head off was from her state, and he was a pretty important person. He had a bunch of important looking pins and honors starting to fall off his lapel as he shook his fists and continued on his tirade. "What are you? A Goddamn fucking moron?!" he screamed at the bus driver. "Let me off this bus right now! Right. The fuck. Now!"

Her state's Republican National Committee chairman had officially lost it. He was banging on the windows of the door demanding that he be let off. His wife, whom he had basically smuggled onto the bus with him because she was not a delegate, simply a spouse, was horrified. She turned her back on her husband to focus her attention on one of the juggling protesters festooned in a tall 'Cat in the Hat' hat and wearing a 'Don't Taze Me Bro!' T-shirt.

The Virginia chairman attempted to intervene and told Jocelyn's chairman to calm down and to treat the driver with some respect. That only threw the whole bus into a tizzy.

"Well, we have been driving around aimlessly for two hours."

"Yeah, you'd think they might have done some practice drive-throughs or something."

"Or at least given the driver a map..."

"Just let the guy off the bus!"

So the driver, thankfully, let the ranting man off the bus. The proud ranter must have assumed everyone would just follow his logic and defiantly march off the bus with him in a show of solidarity, but everyone stayed put as the bus door slammed shut behind him.

Jocelyn was, of course, laughing her butt off now. As much as she wanted to, she couldn't stop. People were eyeing her as she headed down the aisle and attempted to regain her composure in the restroom at the back of the bus. That didn't work. She knew people could hear her laughing uncontrollably from behind the flimsy door, but she didn't care. It was most inappropriate, but what the heck was going on?!

When she emerged from the seclusion of the restroom, she noticed that a drum circle had surrounded the bus. She lost it and burst out laughing again as she headed back to her seat. The bus driver started laying on the horn. This was construed as the exact opposite of 'get out of the way' and seemed to encourage the self-taught percussionists.

"Oh, look, he's doing cartwheels now," the stowaway wife said, commenting on the status of the Cat in the Hat juggler. The female parole officer looked as if she was going to cry now, too. She hopped off the bus with her hand on her pistol, and like the Incredible Hulk, moved a few more Jersey barriers.

They were getting closer.

This was just about the time that the author of the Minority Report and the Rules Committee members on the bus decided it was do or die time. They had the convention center in sight. They asked the bus driver to open the door, and they jumped and ran. The running slowed to a jog and the jog to a walk. Of course, when they finally reached the building, they all had to go through the metal detectors and the credentials checkpoints.

They made the meeting. *Yes!* But missed the vote. *Damn.*

Now it would be up to the party members inside the convention hall to ratify the rules change.

CHAPTER THIRTY-ONE

Meanwhile
North Kingstown, RI
Ethan's house

"THIS IS LOWE." *extended silence* "10-4. I'm on it."

Ethan had to think it through, and the only way he could do this was to offload the kids.

The ambulance showed up in eighteen minutes. Jocelyn's mother was there in thirty. Ethan made the ambulance wait until Jocelyn's mother had arrived. Hugs and kisses and tears all around, and then Ethan slowly crawled onto the stretcher.

"It's probably a kidney stone, ma'am. They'll get him fixed up at the hospital."

"I have my phone, and I'll call you when I can," Ethan gasped as they loaded his clearly fatigued body into the back of the ambulance. The flashing lights were snapped on and off they flew as the kids and their nana held hands and waved goodbye.

"Thanks, guys. You're always there in a pinch," Ethan said appreciatively as he sat up on the stretcher. "I can't thank you enough about that emergency electrical work you guys did."

"That's what we're here for. Believe me, it's not because we like you," the guy dressed as an EMT said. Ethan grinned, took the phone out of his pocket and started messaging.

The ambulance sped off to the hospital where the Medical AirEvac helicopter was waiting for him. The helicopter ride would be the first leg of his journey.

"Back to Zurich," he sighed. "Figures Ledergerber needs

to see me *now*." But it wasn't so bad. SwissAir stewardesses were always a pleasure.

CHAPTER THIRTY-TWO

JOCELYN AND THE OTHER DELEGATES who were not on the Rules Committee got off the bus just in time to meet the alternate delegates and spouses.

"You just got here? We did too!"

As they were swapping stories of their unfortunate drive in, Jocelyn spotted a bunch of frenzied looking delegates almost running past them. One of the frenzied, a young woman, must have heard them complaining about the bus journey and stopped. She told them that the same thing happened to her bus, too.

"No way!"

"Yeah, and we missed the Rules Committee meeting."

"So did we!" Jocelyn said. "And we had the author of the Minority Report on our bus and—"

"Oh, that's perfect! Just perfect," the delegate said in exasperation. "I'm from Iowa, and if they change the rules, we're screwed."

"Well, all right! Iowa! Nice to meet you," Jocelyn shook the woman's hand. "Ray Pierce did really well in Iowa, huh?"

The Iowan nodded. "But if they change the rules..."

They all made their way into the main hall, separated and found their assigned seats. The teleprompter had already been sparked up, and the speakers were droning on. It was funny to watch the orators trying to appear as if they were engaging with the audience or the cameras. Some didn't even bother with the theatrics and made no attempt to hide the fact that they were reading a rolling script off the large blue screens located on the A/V control booth.

The woman seated in front of Jocelyn had, naturally, been on the Delegates Only bus and must have decided that this was the optimal time to get to know Jocelyn better.

"So," she said, making an obvious effort to smile, "you're a Ray Pierce delegate, I hear."

Jocelyn nodded.

"Why did you come here today?"

"What do you mean?" Jocelyn was confused by the question.

"Well, you know he's not going to win."

Nice. Can this woman just turn around and listen to whatever the guy on stage is talking about? The woman continued to stare at her, waiting for an answer.

"I don't think that matters. I was elected to be here. I am representing twenty-five percent of the people who voted in the Republican primary."

The woman chuckled with a rude kind of guffaw. Jocelyn should have just ignored her, but asked, "Who are you here to represent? Rooney?" She knew, but she asked anyway.

The woman smiled and gave a big double thumbs up. "He'll clean up the White House and get this country back on track! He's the only one who can."

"Well, anything would be better than what we have going on now, that's for sure," Jocelyn said and the woman nodded in agreement. The woman finally turned to face the stage but then quickly turned back around.

"So you're going to vote for Rooney? Right?"

"What, today? No. Ray Pierce, of course."

"No. I mean in the General Election."

"Oh, probably Ray Pierce."

Now it was the woman's turn to be confused. She shook her head. "Honey, he's not going to be on the ballot if he isn't nominated at this convention."

"Write-ins count in our state."

Visibly irritated, the woman twisted her weight in the folding chair and leaned on the backrest to fully address Jocelyn. "So by writing him in, you know you'd be voting for the current president. You'd be throwing your vote away."

She grimaced and rolled her eyes. "It's either one or the other. The Marxist sitting in the White House or Rooney."

"I don't particularly care for either one of them. They both have the exact same corporate sponsors."

"Well, the corporations are just hedging their bets. They want to be on the good side of the next president."

"No. It's whoever is behind this whole election that is hedging the bet. It doesn't matter if Rooney gets in or if the current president stays put. Either would be equally acceptable. Sure, lobbyists and contracts would flow to different companies, but it's still a net loss for America."

"Well, let's deal with reality, shall we?"

"Okay. If you insist. The reality is that they both support the idea that government needs to be spending more than we have. They both support war as an economic engine. They both support the erosion of the Bill of Rights and—"

"Yes, but those are our only choices! You have to choose one or the other!"

"No, I don't.

"Yes, you do! Everyone knows you have to pick one!" the flabbergasted woman screeched. Then she stared at Jocelyn as if studying some sort of curious mutant algae in a petri dish. "You're not an American! You don't get it! Why don't you just leave! Get out!" she screamed, flinging her arm up to point to the door.

Seriously? Did she just say I wasn't an American because I wouldn't vote for the lesser of two evils?

Maybe it was because Jocelyn was tired. Or maybe it was because she hadn't eaten anything of nutritional value in three days. Or maybe she was just sick of hearing it and thought this whole election thing was so far removed from solving anyone's problems that she just snapped. Jocelyn, like the mad ranter on the bus, just lost it.

"Oh! Oh! I'm *more* American than half the people you know! Thank you very much! My great, great, great, great, great grandfather, Ebenezer McLaren, dressed up like an

Indian during the original—I said *original!*—Boston Tea Party! And my family..."

At that point, Jocelyn wasn't even sure she knew what she was saying, and she just let it rip. The people around the two of them backed away. Then a few latchers-on felt the need to get involved by shouting soundbites, and it wasn't pretty. A short but intense bout of vein-popping accusations were flying all over the place and were left hanging in the air.

Luckily, Jocelyn had other RP people nearby to calm her down before she had an aneurysm or something. She felt badly that she had handled it that way. She had always prided herself on being the level-headed one. It had been so uncool and totally out of character. Now, as she made the effort to breathe and just let it go, she had a deeper appreciation for the original Ray Pierce MeetUp organizer that everyone had voted off the island, Kris Jung. *It's no wonder that guy was flying off the handle all the time. Flipping tables and all...*

The speaker on the stage was getting ready to talk about the rules change and take the vote that would ratify the changes. It was pretty much the definition of a dog and pony show. The National Chairman read from the teleprompter and quickly breezed over the fact that half the stadium was shouting 'NAY!' and 'No!' A show of hands, or something like that, would have quickly and politely settled the whole thing. Alas, the teleprompter rolled on, and the National Chair kept reading. When the Pierce supporters saw that they were getting steamrolled, they started yelling.

POINT OF ORDER! POINT OF ORDER! POINT OF ORDER!

The room had erupted. USA! USA! began to get chanted, which Jocelyn recognized as the convenient audio cover up when the crowd wasn't behaving. Jocelyn didn't know if the 'USAs' were pre-recorded or not, but she kept yelling, "point of order!" until she just couldn't anymore.

Jocelyn knew enough to know that all the chanting and yelling going on had something to do with <u>*Robert's Rules of*</u>

Order. She only had a vague idea about what 'point of order' really meant, but she saw the other RP delegates on the floor going nuts, shouting it as if their lives depended on it, so she joined in.

Others around her started shouting USA! USA! USA! trying to drown out the 'point of order' cries. It was only Tuesday, and the whole thing was already a disaster.

The gavel was struck. The YEAs had it, and anyone who had made the effort to vote months ago in Virginia, Iowa, Nevada, Minnesota, and Maine—no matter who they voted for—just had their vote crumpled up and thrown away. Ray Pierce's name wouldn't even be allowed to be uttered during the official tabulation of delegate numbers. Rooney's lawyer, along with a complicit crew of 'yes men' (and women), just assured that the current president would enjoy another four years in the White House.

CHAPTER THIRTY-THREE

The next morning
RNC Day Three

THE ALARM CLOCK STARTED BUZZING again. Mišel was dreading going into work. She had never been in one place for so long, and she had no idea how people actually lived like this, or why they would want to. Smacking off the alarm, she hoisted herself out of bed and reminded herself that she would be able to leave after the Republican National Convention. As she moseyed over to the bathroom in her oversized Tampa University T-shirt, she looked around the modest in-law apartment. She had chosen the place because the landlady living in the main house was ancient, hard of hearing, and had pretty bad cataracts. She was the perfect landlord for someone running around with an alias. Mišel's landlady knew her as Michelle Jones, and Mišel was getting pretty sick of carrying that name around. Taking a quick inventory of the tidy 1970s kitchen with its orange and avocado flowered wallpaper, Mišel concluded that this middle-America thing was not the life she was meant for.

How can people live like this? This is torture.

She wanted to get out there and kill someone. That's what she was good at. Or at least used to be good at. Sure, that unexpected meeting with Heartbreaker seemed like it might have been something, but that was a hack job. She hadn't received any instructions other than to "get cooking" and the coordinates and time of the meeting. She only knew it was an official order when it appeared on her desk with a minuscule gold coin. She had been hoping Heartbreaker would clue her in on what the job was when they met, but it seemed like she wasn't talking. At all. She didn't know what to "cook," so she just concocted a very basic poison and passed it on. It was only after she left the International Plaza did it occurred to her that maybe Heartbreaker didn't know why they were meeting either. But that wasn't their style. There were no wasted movements within this organization.

Back only a few years ago, Mišel was on fire. She was offing executives and bankers. The easiest was that woman in Connecticut, that typist Nancy. That was a cinch once she got that target to eat. The woman never ate anything other than crackers, but once she did... Mišel had grabbed those stupid log book entries. That's how she ended up dealing with the congressman who later introduced her to Ledergerber.

She wasn't sure what the congressman had to do with anything other than that his name was listed as the salesman on the pages she handed in. The owner of the company was in on it too or something, and she guessed that woman Nancy was threatening to expose the congressman or ruin the impending sale of the defense company to the Conglomerate. She didn't know and really didn't care, but gleaned that somehow Nancy dropping dead was financially beneficial to both the owner and the congressman. Her final payment came to her on a Darling Vinter's Import/Export check. Crazy. But whatever. The check was good.

As she smeared toothpaste on the toothbrush and was getting ready to pop it into her mouth, she noticed the massively overgrown bougainvillea in the yard. The purplish flowers were getting pelted with rain, and it looked like the bush was swaying unnaturally, but then it stopped. Still holding the toothbrush, she edged closer to the tiny bathroom window and peered out.

"*Probably the hurricane,*" she smirked. She would have been laughing out loud at this comment if she didn't actually hate her stupid job at the Weather Channel so much. It's not like she could call in on account of the weather.

Mišel had been certifiably cooped up as a data entry clerk

for over a year now and had started putting the pieces together when she noticed a steady stream of meteorologists getting laid off, fired, or told it was just time to leave. She had watched with mild interest the build-up of the court case between a woman named Nicole Mitchell, who was a U.S. Air Force Reserve captain and one of the "Hurricane Hunters" team, and the Weather Channel, recently acquired by Bain Capital. The Weather Channel had the highest national distribution of any U.S. cable channel and was a hot property because it was a trusted source.

Mišel had thought that she was going to get assigned to knock off Ms. Mitchell or one of the meteorologists, since it appeared the channel simply did not want hurricane specialists on board. She never got word about a job like that, though. So she just sat there day in and day out, inputting weather reports.

It was drudgery, and she was depressed. She had even started to fantasize about running away. Just disappearing. Becoming a ghost or something, but she knew that they'd eventually find her. Especially because now she knew that what she was inputting everyday was not officially official. She had been following orders and "beefing it up," making it more dramatic for "entertainment purposes." Transforming herself into a ghost because she was bored really wasn't worth the risk. *I'll be out of here soon enough,* she thought as she studied the bags under her eyes in the mirror.

She turned her attention back to the sink, started the water running and began brushing. It was just before Mišel was ready to spit that a single Remington .260 bullet pierced the tiny bathroom window and instantly splashed her brain all over the pink and black bathroom tiles.

CHAPTER THIRTY-FOUR

RNC
Day Three

Black, back seam hosiery. Check.
Black satin gloves. Check.
Black form fitting dress. Check.
And to top it all off, the most charming black Kentucky Derby hat ever.
Checkity, check, check, check!

JOCELYN JUST HAD TO LIVE through two more days. Today and tomorrow. Two more days until the big show. She was getting amped for this. She had everything she needed, except she knew people wouldn't get it. She needed something that spelled it out in no uncertain terms what the heck she was doing. The scene with the buses and the rules change only served as fuel for her fire. What had completely thrown her over the edge and convinced her that she was doing the right thing was seeing not one, but three Carlos Delohim butterfly pins since she got there.

One was on TV. They were interviewing the former First Lady and asking her about the convention. She was wearing one. Another was up by the press boxes inside the convention center. And one was on a woman coming out of the gift shop that was packed exclusively with Team Rooney football jerseys, sweatshirts, baseball hats, shot glasses, you name it. If it was made in China and could have a Team Rooney logo printed on it, it was in there. Jocelyn had been so astounded to see that butterfly walking out of that tourist trap of a shop, that she felt compelled to stop the woman and ask her about it.

"Oh, excuse me," Jocelyn had asked when she caught up to the woman. "I have to comment on that brooch. It caught my eye from way over there, and I love it. It's just... just amazing." She then proceeded to fall into a ridiculously long conversation with the lady. (The brooch-woman was obviously not from the Northeast; she was far too friendly). It turned out, the woman was from California. She was buying a Team Rooney ashtray for her elderly mother who had been to every single Republican National Convention since before Goldwater. The lady confirmed that the name of the designer of her pin was Carlos Delohim. Although the butterfly itself was slightly different because of the jewels used, Jocelyn could tell it was an original. She also saw the little pentagrams on it. Obviously, it was in style.

Thinking about that exchange with the lady outside the gift shop, Jocelyn considered how out of the loop she was a far as current fashion was concerned. She looked at the black clothes arranged on the other queen bed. Memories of Tim Brucker and his last words to her before his car vaporized swirled around in her head. *Why did he think that pin would save my life?* The dude was obviously involved with some serious money, but she didn't know if he was a good guy or a bad guy. Anyhow, she didn't have the butterfly pin anymore. The FBI did. Would she have worn it if she had it? Maybe, but probably not. The clothes on the other bed were solidifying themselves in her mind as funerary items.

She was getting sidetracked. She wanted to carry out her personal mission. If the convention was this much of a shit show, oh, rest assured she would put on a show, too. She tried to compose some sort of statement about why she wanted to dress up and do this. She had already made up her mind that she was going to print it out on business cards. That way all she had to do was walk around, look stunning, catch someone's eye and then leave them with a message to think about as she walked away.

It was basically, in her mind, performance art. Ethan had once said to her, and she remembered it well, "If you are so upset, write a song or paint a picture. At least you'll have something to show for it." Of course, he had sort of yelled that, but the message was the same, only missing exclamation points. So this was her creative solution, and she finally felt like she was doing something proactive.

CHAPTER THIRTY-FIVE

Meanwhile
East Haddam, Connecticut

JERRY WASN'T UPSET. He was frantic. He had been watching it on TV, and he knew. He just knew there was going to be an 'incident' in Tampa during the RNC. How did he know? Because, of course, he hadn't made one backup copy of the ChemTrailTales server. He had a bunch. Each time he updated ChemTrailTales with new photos and eyewitness accounts, he would do a backup of the entire machine. Sure, he didn't have the latest comments posted at the website about the Air Force's Air University strategy paper *Weather as a Force Multiplier: Owning the Weather in 2025*, but he did have copies of everything else that had been stored on that computer until it got stolen. He had made it his life's work since he had last seen Jocelyn to find out what exactly that server had been holding.

Brucker had tons of stuff on there. He included scans of business cards and handwritten notes. The thing with the race car in Italy was fascinating and had occupied a lot of Jerry's time. Especially the part about where Brucker's cut of the money was to be deposited. It was a place called the Institute per le Opere de Religione (Institute of the Works of Religion), otherwise known as the IOR. The IOR was one of a few "untouchable" banks located within the Vatican. Jerry had spent a long time rooting through that information not only because he had been brought up Catholic and this thing with the various Vatican banks surprised him, but because it appeared that the file containing photos of the butterfly jewelry was linked to that IOR account as well.

Communications that Brucker had saved around that IOR topic included conversations—brief messages, really—(Jerry had learned a long time ago that the brief messages were the ones you had to look out for) indicating that someone Brucker was working over (a.k.a. blackmailing) was going to put the smackdown on the whole extortion thing once and for all at the Republican National Convention. This plan was a win-win for the pissed-off 'victim' of Brucker's blackmail scheme. Not only was it going to eliminate further irritation caused by Brucker, it would also enhance shareholder value by being such a public display of homicidal lunacy.

Of course, this threat on the backup disc was from almost five months ago. Maybe it wasn't even going to happen. Given what he knew about Jocelyn, however, he was afraid for her. He had to warn her or get her out of there.

CHAPTER THIRTY-SIX

Tampa, Florida

JOCELYN HAD TAKEN DAY THREE OFF. There was no point in going into that convention today. Like, who wants to sit around and listen to every single kicked-to-the curb Republican presidential candidate? The RNC was behaving like RP didn't even exist, and the press, although showing weak glimmers of skepticism about this gag order, was playing right along.

By not going to the convention hall, Jocelyn had many options available to her. She had been invited to go to Six Flags amusement park with some other completely non-plussed delegates. Or antiquing with some Rooney wives. She had also been invited to a movie screening hosted by a previous female National Security Advisor about kids and public schools. *Really?*

She didn't want to go to that, but the invitation intrigued her. It was apparent that they were pulling on any X chromosome they could find in order to illustrate that they were actively engaging the 'Women's Vote." The co-host was some female politician from Australia.

Jocelyn looked the woman up. She was a member of the International Democrat Union (IDU). *Oh, how odd. A Democrat from another country featured at the RNC?* Jocelyn didn't know what the IDU was, so she had looked that up, too, and was surprised to find that the Republican Party in the United States was a member of this international, self-described center right, Christian coalition. Former Republican Vice President (at the time), George H.W. Bush started this organization. *Interesting. So a Republican vice president starts up an international Democrat Union... hmmm.*

She wondered about all the speeches and soundbites that were being transmitted all over the world. The ones where a U.S. president would get up and talk about the importance of spreading Democracy. How was that being translated and understood? She also wondered, uncomfortably, whether people in far flung third world countries perceived the actions of Americans as the direct product of Christianity. *Probably. Gee... I wonder if the Democrats are part of the International Republican Union?*

Although that made her smirk, she didn't think that it was true, but honestly, it wouldn't surprise her at this point. The way that words got twisted around. Heck, the term 'conservative' in American politics used to mean what we currently call 'liberal.' So the term Neo-Con actually means... It made Jocelyn's head hurt to think about that one.

No. Jocelyn wasn't going to any movie, or amusement park, or poking around looking at deceased retirees' furniture. She was hard at work at the local copy shop producing the stuff she was going to need for tomorrow's Coronation. She was in her element, and it felt good.

That night she figured she should bulk up on real food. That way she'd have the energy to pull this off. The past few days, she had been starting to feel dizzy. She refused to entertain the idea that it might be due to her M.S. She ate a nutritious dinner at the Greek restaurant across the street from the hotel.

While finishing her dinner in silence, she realized that she was really missing her kids. So she walked over to the gift shop and bought some souvenirs for them.

After her purchase of the overpriced stuffed dolphin and magnetic rocks was complete, she headed back to her room. She plopped her laptop on her pillow and learned to say 'hello' and 'thank you' in Arabic, Farsi, French, German, Italian, Mandarin and Polish. She already knew how to say it in Russian and Spanish. She figured if the U.S. press avoided her, then she'd set her sights on the foreign press. Everyone—I don't care who you are—likes to at least hear 'hello' and 'thank you' in their own language.

She did that until she fell asleep.

CHAPTER THIRTY-SEVEN

Meanwhile
Union Station
New Haven, Connecticut, USA

JERRY COVERED THE MOUTHPIECE and studied the nasty scribbles on the wall as the next arrival was announced. Then he leaned into the pay phone for added privacy and whispered, "Gino, dude, seriously? That's all you've got?" Jerry was basically begging his ex-fiancé's brother for help. He was convinced that Jocelyn was in deep shit. If he had been able to break into Ethan's house and crack the gun safe, he probably would have done that. Not that he would have known how to actually handle those guns. At least it would look impressive—you know, in a pinch, that's really what matters.

"You mean to tell me, that's all your dad has?"

"Well, that's all I can get for you on this short notice, Jerry. I mean, you get what you pay for. This thing has some balls. It will get the job done."

Jerry sighed. "Gino, your dad's in the mafia, isn't he?"

"Jesus, Jerry! Not on the phone! No! Not at all. He operates a legitimate import/export business with distribution through eBay. Totally above board. So you gonna take this baby? Or what?"

"That *thing* is totally *not* what I was looking for, Gino."

"You can travel with it, Jerry. Totally legal. I'll even drive it over."

Jerry pressed his lips together for a moment, then sighed and said, "Fine. I'll take it."

He hadn't really been imagining himself rescuing Jocelyn

wielding a military-grade flamethrower.

CHAPTER THIRTY-EIGHT

RNC
Day Four

THE NEXT MORNING Jocelyn woke up an hour before her alarm, which was set for an hour before she would have normally set it. She had a lot of nervous energy, but she was focused. She had a sense of purpose, and doing this was going to make the whole trip down here worth it. Even if her piece of performance art only impacted one person—*just one person*—she would consider it a success.

As she showered that morning, she practiced her language skills some more. Then she took her time getting ready, doing her hair and makeup just so. Jocelyn really wasn't much of a makeup person, but today she focused on looking naturally sultry. She wiggled into the form-hugging black dress. It fit perfectly. Very flattering. The hardest part of the whole ensemble was getting the seams straight on the stockings. *No wonder nobody wears these things anymore. Jeeze...* She slipped on the high wedges. Slid the silky black gloves up her arms. Finally, as if placing the crown on a winning beauty queen, she donned the hat that had inspired this whole scheme.

Of course, she was two hours early.

She sat on her bed facing the large mirror that all hotel rooms have and read the business cards that she had made up.

I am here today to offer my condolences

to the United States of America

because her citizens are no longer thinking like Americans.

Instead, her people are being manipulated into following
one of two political parties,
which will ultimately benefit a very small
percentage of individuals.
The current two party system does not represent or benefit
We The People.

Please know that I am not speaking on behalf of any
party or politician.

And on the back (yes, it was double sided on the cheapest 110-lb. card stock) just to drive the point home:

"Beware of political parties."
-George Washington
Farewell address, 1797

Washington pleaded for American political neutrality,
that citizens not be forced to choose
between political alternatives, but rather choose their leaders
on the basis of merit and reputation.

She thought they looked good. She read them over and over again as she fussed with how the cards would fit into her dainty little Jessica McClintock purse. The purse looked like an elegant, black silk-covered pint of ice cream with four black silk roses on the lid. It had a little satin loop so that she could carelessly sway it while she walked. She was just realizing that she had had this thing since her Junior Prom.

Anyway, after straightening her back seams and adjusting the hat again, she went downstairs and hung out in the lobby. Because nobody was taking those convention buses anymore, she waited almost two hours for a ride. By the time she and the person driving the rental car headed out, she was over being dressed like she was going to a funeral. But she was committed to the project and checked herself in the visor mirror again.

The driver, Carl, was older than her. In his sixties, an RP delegate and a delegate on the state's Central Committee, he instantly got what she was doing. He didn't even need the card, but he took one and put it in his jacket pocket anyway. During the course of the drive, he talked about how he felt down in Tampa. A lot of what he had believed about the process of voting had just gotten thrown out the window, and he was really depressed.

"The thing is, Jocelyn, what are you gonna do?" Carl began. "I mean, those rules that just got ratified, the Democrats have had the same provisions in their rules for a few years now, too."

Interesting.

"And what? Okay, like maybe there is an unknown third party out there with a candidate that I really like. But he doesn't have a chance to even get in the ring to compete. The D's and the R's have it locked up."

Jocelyn's mind wandered as she watched the Florida shoreline scroll through the window, and she thought about her kids at home. How they never wanted to wear a sweater. How they would insist that they weren't chilly, and how she would have to coerce them to accept the sweater by distracting them with the illusion of choice.

"I don't want to wear a sweater."

"But look, you can have a red one *or* a blue one!"

"I'm not cold. It makes me all scratchy."

"But you have to pick one. Red's nice. I like red. Which color is your favorite?"

"Blue."

"Great! I like blue, too!"

Then the sweater, for the child's own good, would instantly be pulled over the kid's head.

"Good choice! You look awesome!"

Mission accomplished.

Yeah... she was sad, too. Sitting in the car all dolled up as if going to funeral, she realized that she was growing up. She felt as if she was saying goodbye to a long-time, childhood make-believe friend. The illusion of choice was slowly evaporating in this Florida heat.

CHAPTER THIRTY-NINE

Meanwhile

"YEAH. UMM. I'm here to see Jocelyn McLaren," Jerry said as he glanced around the hotel lobby. It wasn't like the other hotel where all the other Rhode Island delegates were staying. That place was really nice. Like, over two hundred dollars a night nice. Enormously impressive. When he showed up over there to track her down, after taking the most expensive Southwest Airlines flight ever to Tampa, he found out that Rhode Island was one of the few states that did not require all their delegates stay at the hotel that the RNC had assigned them. So he started asking around for nearby cheap hotels and ended up here. It was right on the beach next to a nightclub featuring palm trees covered with colorful, flashing, Christmas tree lights.

"Do you have her room number?"

"Ahh... No," Jerry said as he leaned on the reception desk. "Jocelyn McLaren. Tall chick with reddish hair. Super friendly."

The man behind the desk smiled as he typed the name into the computer. "Was she going to a funeral today?"

The comment stunned Jerry. What did this guy know? Was he part of the plot? "Jesus, I hope not," he blurted. "But she's here?"

The reception manager raised his eyebrows and looked up.

"No. She just left about fifteen minutes ago."

"Was she with anyone? I need to find her." Thinking it through, he added, "It's a family emergency."

"Well, I believe she left with an older man. They had a

red rental."

"Do you have the license plate number back there anywhere?"

"Uhmmm... I'm not at liberty to share that with you."

"God damn it! I just told you this was a family emergency!" Jerry was really fired up. His acting skills were improved greatly because he actually was freaking out. At last, the guy behind the counter, knowing that Jocelyn had appeared to be going to funeral, figured that Jerry might not know about the death and broke down and gave him the plate number.

"Thanks!" Jerry said as he slapped his hand on the counter and ran out.

He jumped back into his rental car, consulted his GPS and set off to the RNC.

CHAPTER FORTY

"OH, FOR GOODNESS SAKE! We were just here!" Carl exclaimed. They had followed the directions of the traffic rent-a-cops and ended up driving around the perimeter of the entire stadium, only to emerge back on the road they had been on but heading in the opposite direction. Jocelyn was in charge of the map and looking for clues. Carl read every visible sign aloud, and finally they were flagged into a parking garage. It was then that their journey really began in earnest. "Could they have picked a parking garage any farther away from the stadium? Jeeze," Carl huffed as the two of them plodded off toward the convention center.

After about two blocks, one of the rent-a-cops told them that a shuttle would be coming down this way soon and if they would just wait, they could jump on that and avoid the walk.

So they waited. Jocelyn proudly gave the very first of her business cards to the rent-a-cop. However, she didn't realize that she would be standing there awkwardly, festooned in full-on funeral garb for approximately fifteen minutes. It was painful, to say the least.

Finally, the rent-a-cop broke the silence and told them the shuttle was right down the street. The two eager conference goers edged out to the curb.

"Uh... I don't see it," said Jocelyn.

"It's right there," the rent-a-cop gestured.

Jocelyn and her companion stepped out into the road and looked around.

"Where?" asked Carl.

"Right there!" he said, pointing emphatically and making an expression which was easily discernible as meaning 'who are these assholes?'

They still didn't see a shuttle bus. They were pretty sure the guy was playing a trick on them until a white golf cart emblazoned with the Team Rooney logo pulled up.

Jocelyn immediately marveled at the amount of money being spent on branding for this event. Ashtrays, shot glasses, football jerseys and now a golf cart. Make that at least thirty golf carts. It became apparent that the roadways behind the Jersey barriers were fully stocked with Team Rooney carts whizzing up and down and across the streets.

Their golf cart already had three passengers. But if Jocelyn held onto her hat, squeezed in between the driver and the other guy riding shotgun, and if Carl stood on the tail, held onto one of the poles that supported the roof, and hung on for dear life, they'd get there. No problem.

The five passengers arrived at their destination and hopped off the Team Rooney cart.

"Now where do we go?" asked one of the ladies who had ridden in the back. Jocelyn later concluded that this same woman was clearly a genius because she had worn sneakers with her Talbots skirt. Jocelyn's ankles were absolutely screaming at this point.

"Over there," the volunteer driver smiled as she pointed to a white tent. "Enter right there." Everyone thanked the volunteer and crawled through the flap of the tent. Once their eyes became accustomed to the light, they could see that the pathway, covered by white tenting, was lined with red carpet. Every twenty feet, an enormous, five-foot-diameter hanging arrangement composed exclusively of lush, red roses was suspended from the ceiling of the tent. As Jocelyn marveled at the line of floral tributes, trying to estimate the cost of just one, they arrived at a zippered flap. Carl opened it up and exclaimed, "Good Lord! This goes on forever!" For as far the eye could linearly see, the red carpet extended, and a floribunda of red roses graced the ceiling. Jocelyn decided to take off her shoes.

As they got closer, they had to go up some steps. Jocelyn realized that she was starting to feel weaker. She grabbed the flimsy red velvet piping for support as she climbed up. When she and Carl got to the top, there was another zipper flap. "It keeps going!" Carl proclaimed in amazement. Only this time, in addition to the red carpet, centered in between each of the giant, hanging rose arrangements, there was a large monolith—like something out of 2001: A Space Odyssey or a hip international airport—that housed a video monitor looping ads for things like: Lipitor; a home diabetes test; Verizon - Can You Hear Me Now?; Pork - the other white meat; Viagra; and something Jocelyn never really figured out. Harley Davidson, maybe?

Anyway, this mystery visual was a really long, well-produced thing featuring a handsome retiree dramatically riding a motorcycle in slow motion at a high rate of speed though a desert. That was her favorite ad. The overall vibe was "Independence" and "Freedom" and "being in control of your own destiny." Because she had seen it looped now at least fifteen times and she still didn't know what it was for, she decided that the Verizon ad was better and figured that maybe the motorcycle thing was just to get people into the mood psychologically for the convention.

"We should have packed a canteen for this," Carl said. He was going to say something else, but an older, heavyset man, whom they guessed later must have been from Texas because of his accent, passed them going in the opposite direction. He was speaking really loudly into his cell phone, "Look, darlin', it's not you. It's just bad timing. If I wasn't married..."

Carl and Jocelyn quickly caught each other's glance, and Carl said, "Well, it sounds like we're getting closer."

Finally, they got to the metal detectors, which were a breeze. She just had to put her purse in a tray and have it checked out. She was nervous that the guard was going to confiscate her business cards, but he couldn't have cared less.

Then they hiked up some more stairs, and they were in!

"Want a water or something?" visibly sweaty Carl asked Jocelyn, who was putting on her shoes again.

Jocelyn eagerly accepted, and they both sat down to chug the water. They noticed from the window that huge screens had been erected outside. Both screens were broadcasting, in tandem, the speech going on inside. Right now, one of the kicked-to-the curb candidates was crying. That's right, crying. His tears were running down his fifty-foot-tall cheeks as he emotionally declared his love of country, party, and his developmentally disabled child. The camera was panning in on the women in the audience as they dabbed away their tears and nodded in agreement.

"Really going for that 'Women's Vote' I guess, huh?" Jocelyn commented shaking her head at how corny it was.

"It would seem so. So, where do you want to start?"

"Down on the floor, I guess."

There was almost no one in there. You'd never know it from the big screens outside, but then again, it didn't surprise her. The state delegation areas were only one-third full at best. The stands were at about the same capacity. Jocelyn set her sights on Hawaii first. She sauntered over to a bunch of women who were giddily passing out leis.

"Aloha!" said a woman as she attempted to hang the garland of flowers around Jocelyn's neck. It wouldn't fit over the hat, and the woman just handed it to her.

"Aloha. This is lovely. Thank you. Did you make it?" Jocelyn asked, inspecting the lei.

"Oh, no. Alemea ordered them up at a local florist."

"Your hat is amazing!" commented another woman. "I love it. You didn't make that, did you?"

"Oh, no, but I made these." With her black-gloved hand, she plucked five cards out of her dainty little purse. She gave one to each of the five women with a smile and moseyed off to hit the next delegation.

Same M.O. She chatted up a bunch of ladies about their

jewelry and how they fared during the 'hurricane' when the RNC was called off. During the chat backs, she began to notice that not one person knew what all the shouting had been about the other day. They were clueless regarding the Rules change, so Jocelyn took it upon herself to educate them. "Yeah, so now the presumptive nominee can just snatch up any old elected delegate he wants and replace them with whoever..."

"Oh, that's what that was all about?"

"No. It was about those Ray Pierce people wanting to cause a scene!" interrupted another. "I just can't stand them! They are so rude!"

"I wouldn't be so sure," corrected Jocelyn. "Fine, this election it's Team Rooney picking the delegates. But unless we oppose this, next election, if these rules still stand, it might be Team Hitler. Who knows?" She handed them each a business card and wandered off.

Jocelyn looked back to make sure Carl was still trailing her like a private eye, making sure that she was all right. He gave her a thumbs up, and she turned away to hit another delegation. Just then, a woman wearing a lei came running up to her.

"Here! Take these back!" she said, extending a trembling hand and offering Jocelyn's business cards back to her. "We don't want anything to do with this!" Jocelyn nodded and took them back. The woman yanked the lei that Jocelyn had wrapped around her wrist. The chain of flowers broke and tumbled to the floor. People turned to stare, and the Hawaiian woman ran off.

Carl had been watching and gave her a thumbs down and pointed to the exit.

Jocelyn nodded and headed out. Carl met her in front of the McDonald's where people decorated with Team Rooney pins and cowboy hats were waiting in line for $6.00 burgers.

"What was up with that lady? She looked like she was going nuts."

Jocelyn gave Carl the overview. He nodded.

"So what do you want to do next?"

"I think I should stay up here and hit the press."

Jocelyn, with Carl trailing her, wandered around and said hello to people. If they approached her, she would give them a card and wander off. She spoke to every news organization that she came across. As nothing attracts a camera like a bunch of cameras, soon Jocelyn was giving interviews.

After one interview, a skinny, twenty-something-ish man in a white oxford shirt and rolled-up sleeves walked up to her and really, like really, started hitting on her. It was obnoxious, and Jocelyn thought that he might have been on cocaine; but then again, she had designed it so that she would look attractive. She offered him a card, smiled and then started walking away. She noticed Carl motioning to her. He was spinning his finger like he was stirring cake mix. She turned around. The obnoxious man jammed a cell phone in her face and took a picture.

"Hey! That's not polite." She said, still smiling but shocked nonetheless. She had learned a long time ago that she could often avert tragedy by smiling. The guy took another picture. *What the?* Jocelyn noticed that he was not wearing the normal RNC credentials around his neck. His had a funky border around it and said something about some Israeli meeting group. *How odd?*

"Why aren't you wearing proper credentials?" Jocelyn asked. That made him put his camera down.

"Because I'm not like *you,*" he said with a smirk. "Next time you're in Chicago, look me up. I'll show you and the kids a good time." He turned on his heel and scurried away.

That stunned Jocelyn. Show me *and the kids* a good time? Was the guy just being a twenty-something, cracked-out douche? She turned to look at Carl who was now nowhere to be seen. She started walking over to where she had last seen him stirring cake mix. As she rounded the bend, another man, this one fully suited up, jammed a cell phone in her face too, snapped a picture and said, “Nice hat,” as he quickly entered one of the press boxes and closed the door behind him.

Now she was just flying solo around the outer ring of the convention, the area that housed all the press boxes. She tried knocking on some of the doors. CNN. NBC. FOX. No one would answer. A man, obviously a journalist because he was running with papers in his hand, passed her. She held out a card as he scuttled by, and he took it on the fly. She saw him reading it. He turned around and came back to her.

“I love it,” he said, nodding in agreement.

Jocelyn was thrilled. “So you gonna do a story on it?”

“It doesn’t fit the pre-scripted narrative. Sorry.” He handed her his business card and scooted into one of the press boxes. She looked at the card he had just given her. He was the managing editor at The Blaze. *Glenn Beck’s new thing? Figures.*

Now all she wanted to do was leave. She couldn’t even feel her feet and ankles anymore, they hurt so badly. *Where the heck is Carl?*

Suddenly, it was silent, but something was approaching. Eventually, it took form, and she could hear angry chanting. A determined group of about seventy delegates (or more correctly, de-frocked Ray Pierce delegates) and their supporters were marching through the hall. They all had black arm bands on. Some of the arm bands had an image of Ray Pierce silkscreened on them.

“Oh, Jesus. Did Ray Pierce die?” Jocelyn asked one of the group as they passed by.

“No.” The young woman was amped in the way that only a protestor gets—happy but mad. Full of purpose. Jocelyn knew it well. “Are you the Black Widow? I’ve heard about you!”

The guy marching next to the woman recognized Jocelyn from the late-night, flyers-under-hotel-room-doors stuffing campaign and said, “She’s LadyLiberty70!” and the girl gave

Jocelyn a thumbs up as the collective continued on its march.

"Oh, *you're* the Black Widow!" a husky woman in an ill-fitting Dress Barn suit barked.

Jocelyn turned around. The Dress Barn woman pushed her, and because of her ankles and the shoes, it didn't take much to knock Jocelyn off her feet. Amazingly, the hat was still stuck to her head. Stunned, she looked up at the barking Dress Barn lady. *What the hell?!*

Dress Barn Lady, clearly surprised by her own strength but nevertheless determined to exorcize this demon from her convention, threw one of the 'Beware of Political Parties' business cards in Jocelyn's face. "Get out! You and all your friends, just get out! We are trying to save you, for goodness sake, and all you're doing is causing a scene!"

Jocelyn was pretty sure that statement could have just as easily been directed to Dress Barn Lady by one of the defrocked Ray Pierce delegates.

"Did you just assault that woman?" Jocelyn heard from behind her. She was still too astonished by the whole thing to attempt to stand.

Dress Barn Lady's attention shifted from her weak-ankled victim to the man who was racing toward her.

Another man, near Dress Barn Woman, pushed his way forward to defend her. "Back off, asshole!"

"Did you just call me an asshole?!"

And so went the timeless introduction to a fist fight, complete with women yelling in vain to stop and other men stepping in to try and reason. But today, with the inclusion of the RNC security guards, aided by the backup of Tampa's militarized police, this simple, age-old ritual escalated into something much more than your basic just-fight-it-out-then-go-get-a-beer situation.

Jocelyn sat and watched as The People started battling each other. It was a good thing that part of the group was wearing those black arm bands. It made it easier to spot who was on which team. It wasn't until Jocelyn saw the tasers coming out that she felt the need to crawl away.

The security guards turned into police, and the police turned into riot-geared RoboCops. The whole expanse of the convention hallway morphed into a mass of flailing bodies and began to take on the epic proportions of a Baroque oil painting.

Jocelyn took shelter next to a cement garbage can. She noticed that every time someone took out a camcorder to film the scene, one of the RoboCops would instantly emerge and knock it to the ground. Pretty soon, she began to wonder why the news cameras weren't there filming. After all, they were right there by the entrance to all the press boxes.

"Not part of the pre-scripted narrative."

Jocelyn soon realized that this was probably the optimal location for all this to happen. If this melee happened in front of the McDonald's selling overpriced fast food downstairs, word would have spread quicker than you can say: two all-beef patties special sauce lettuce cheese pickles onions on a sesame seed bun. Everybody knows that. There would have been no containing the news from spreading when real people were actually talking to each other. Here, literally in front of the major media outlets' front doors, well, that was a different story.

"Carl! Carl!" Jocelyn yelled. "Carl!" She saw him bouncing around, and she waved. She couldn't tell if he saw her or not because he was too busy defending himself, but it didn't matter. The zip-ties had already come out.

CHAPTER FORTY-ONE

Meanwhile, up on the convention center ceiling rafters

HEARTBREAKER WAS READY TO ROLL, but something was wrong. She put her finger to her ear and spoke into the sleeve of her Women's Under Armour turtleneck. "Please tell me, please, are we still on hold?"

"That's affirmative. No joy. Repeat: No joy."

The melee had interfered with the plans and had inadvertently saved some lives. There wasn't enough time to get the riot-geared cops in position for the cameras and her well-placed bullets. It was either abort or move her setup two blocks over. Not that that would be hard for her, because it wouldn't. But it wouldn't be a clean getaway, and the cameras would be aimed all over the place and the messaging might be confused because of the Ray Pierce thing in the hall.

Today the point wasn't to create speculation. That's always helpful, of course, but not what they were looking for. Today's operation was to simply hit a few specific targets and leave the audience with the impression that the terrorists or, at the very least, George Soros, FOX News' favorite evil billionaire, was behind the attack.

As Heartbreaker picked up her gear, she sighed. She wasn't necessarily disappointed that the gig was called off, but she was experiencing that thing when you feel like you have to sneeze and you never really get to achieve the sneeze. Yeah, that. Not devastating or life-altering. Just not fulfilling.

She packed up her stuff and decided to go shopping. She sighed again. *Probably just as well*, she thought as she exited the building. She knew they'd call her back when they had her position secured. She'd get her shot soon..

CHAPTER FORTY-TWO

At the police station

"SO WHAT BRINGS YOU HERE?" a barnacle fixed to the only bench in the holding tank managed to slur. Jocelyn honestly wondered the same thing as her weary but still proud gaze began the obligatory study of the shell of a human with whom she was incarcerated. This checking each other out moment lasted much longer than a reasonably comfortable exchange, but seeing as reason was now questionable at best, the unabashed staring was in full effect. "You get in a fight at a funeral or something?"

"Not exactly."

"They caught you hooking?"

Momentarily disoriented by the suggestion, Jocelyn remained outwardly composed as the urge to laugh uncontrollably began to well up.

"Okay, Miss America, you're up next," a tall, clean-shaven, puffed-up-on-steroids police officer announced authoritatively. "The phone's yours now. You can make your call."

That killed the laughter thing. She slipped off her high heels, which were killing her, picked them up, and headed down the hall escorted by Officer Puffy, who offered to hold her shoes. She felt defeated without the hat and now the shoes... Oh, what did it matter anyway? Her gig was over.

Cradling the telephone with one hand, Jocelyn dialed the only phone number that had managed to stay stuck in her memory bank. She was hopeless with numbers. Just hopeless. Numbers and names never seemed to stick when they were supposed to. But she knew this number. She gingerly fingered her swollen lip as she waited for her call to connect.

"This is Ethan Lowe."

"It's me. Where are you?"

"Switzerland."

"Again? Are the kids with you?"

"No, they're with your mother. But where are you?"

"I got arrested. I'm at the police station—"

He cut her off. "Oh, man, Joss. I can't do much from here. Do you need money? I can try and wire—"

Now she cut him off. "No, I don't need money. Since this is my *only* phone call, can you somehow get in touch with Samantha Ballentine for me? Tell her I've been arrested. She'll know what to do."

"Okay, Joss. Do you have her number?"

"Ummm..." Jocelyn shot a glance over at Officer Puffy. "No, and I'm pretty sure it's unlisted."

"Great."

"Oh, you're back. That was quick," the barnacle said after she cleared her cigarette-grizzled throat.

"I guess so," was Jocelyn's overly courteous response. She was wondering how long she would have to share the cell with this woman when Ms. Barnacle piped up, "So, you gonna tell me your story? Everyone always tells me theirs when I'm in here."

Now, Jocelyn wasn't really into talking to this clearly impaired person, but the question did make her realize that "her story" really started about five years ago—maybe even before that. Yeah, eight years ago was more like it. *Damn. It's been that long?* "Oh, man," she mumbled to herself and checked for a wristwatch that wasn't there.

Obviously displeased with the absence of a story, the Barnacle stretched herself upright on the bench, took matters into her own hands, and began her soliloquy. "Okay, I'll start. First off, I'm not a troublemaker. I quit drinking." *Not likely,* thought Jocelyn. "My neighbors don't like me. That bitch and her boyfriend..." And on it went for almost three-quarters of an hour while Jocelyn politely nodded and tried to figure out if the woman's voice reminded her more of Janis Joplin, Kathleen Turner or Demi Moore. When it all wound down, the silence was almost as disturbing as the unbridled rambling of the story that had just been spun.

Fortunately for all involved, the uncomfortable quiet was short-lived. The front doors of the police station split open, and at least twenty boisterous, riot-gear outfitted paramilitary types simultaneously converged, filling the open space with their presence. It was obvious that the group was trying to constrain some sort of bottled-up energy behind a veneer of professionalism. They all talked over each other as Officer Puffy produced clipboards with appropriate paperwork attached.

"Well?"

"Well, what?"

"I told you mine; now you owe me yours. That's how it works. We're gonna be in here a while, you know."

Trying to hear herself think over the prevailing cacophony of the post-raid fervor, Jocelyn concluded that this woman was correct. They were all going to be here for quite a while.

"Well? How 'bout it? How does your story start?"

Only half-hearing the repeated request from her cellmate and fixating on the black-clad, undulating mass formerly recognizable as riot police, Jocelyn replied in a barely audible murmur, "It was when I found that friggin' gold coin..."

CHAPTER FORTY-THREE

JERRY HAD BEEN CIRCLING the convention center for over two hours and was running out of gas. "This is insane!" Jerry shouted to no one in particular. "Who designed this traffic pattern?"

After narrowly avoiding a potentially fatal crash with a Team Rooney golf cart, he decided to pull into the clearly marked 'do not enter' bus entrance and ask somebody where the nearest gas station was. Buses and a few limousines were parked nose to tail in the enormous parking lot, which led directly to an entrance otherwise called 'backstage.' Jerry spotted a limousine that looked as if it was trying to either pull out or parallel park with the other limousines. He drove over to it and basically cornered it by pulling up right next to it. He rolled down his window.

"Hey! Do you know where the nearest gas station is?!"

The chauffeur yanked his thumb over his shoulder and gave a street address. Jerry took out his GPS and started plugging in the address. "Do you mind?!" the driver shouted as he threw up his hands.

"Huh?"

"Moving your car? See those people coming out right now?" He pointed to a small cluster of people exiting the building. They were gathered around a man in a suit and a woman in what must have been a custom tailoring job. The red form-fitting suit fit like it was made exclusively for her. Jerry didn't notice it. He was too busy looking at something else, but if Jocelyn had been there, she would have seen it immediately. The striking woman was wearing a Carlos Delohim brooch.

Jerry squinted and said, "Hey, one of those guys looks

exactly like the marketing director at the place I use to work at—Robert King. And that guy! I think that used to be my congressman!"

"It probably is. Now would you please move your ass?"

"Oh, sure. No problem."

Jerry pulled his car out of the way and watched as the limousine drove over to Stan and his female friend.

"Wait a minute. Stan's a Democrat. What's he doing here?" thought Jerry. Following his curiosity, he decided to tail the limo because by now it was pretty obvious that he wasn't going to find Jocelyn inside the convention hall. Heck, he couldn't even find a place to park.

The traffic was thick around the convention center. He drove slowly and stayed two cars behind the limo. He had seen that on TV, and it seemed like a good idea. "That chauffeur was probably trained in defensive driving. I've got to be cool about this." Jerry kept his eyes locked on the limo while clicking through the Christian rock and political talk on the radio. When Billy Squire's *Everybody Wants You* started pumping through the speakers, he felt like a character in a movie, and he really got into it. That was until the fuel light began to flicker and Jerry's car started to stutter.

Deciding that it was now or never, Jerry got into the breakdown lane and stepped on the gas. The car lurched ahead of the slow moving traffic, wedged itself right in front of the limousine and promptly ran out of gas. Car horns started honking and beeping as the traffic came to a standstill. Jerry put on his hazard lights and hopped out of his economy rental car. He stood right next to the limo's left front tire and waved the traffic around the obstruction. The limo driver rolled down his window and was yelling for Jerry to get the fuck out of the way.

"What?" Jerry called back, one hand cupped to his ear, the other hand directing traffic. "I can't hear you! I'm out of gas! I can't move!"

When traffic had effectively started on its new course

around the two cars, Jerry walked up to the limousine's rear window and knocked on it. He waited and knocked again. Finally, the tinted glass window slid down revealing Stan the Congressman's patented public persona smiling face.

"Stan! It was you!" Jerry shot out his hand to shake Stan's, and like any good politician, Stan shook it. It became all too evident within the next few seconds that Stan had no idea who Jerry was.

"You remember. Jerry Apario! I used to work at Adam's place, then we got bought by the Conglomerate and..."

"Oh, Adam! Of course! How is that man? Last I heard, he was keeping himself scarce somewhere in the Caribbean on that sailboat of his."

The cars were snaking past Jerry as he spoke. "I have no idea. I thought you were a Democrat, Stan. What are you doing at the RNC?"

Stan chuckled. "A good politician never misses a good party. I heard that some friends of mine were going to be down here and thought I'd swing by and say hello. What brings you?"

"Oh, I have a friend down here, too. Jocelyn McLaren. You remember her."

The woman sitting next to Stan seemed suddenly, nonchalantly interested, and Stan seemed suddenly overtly obtuse. "You didn't happen to call Jocelyn a few months ago? Did you? You know, page her on her beeper?"

The woman in the red suit rolled her eyes while Stan wholeheartedly denied it.

"But you remember her? Right, Stan? I know you know what I'm talking about."

"Ah, Jaaahcelyn..."

A car honked its horn, but Jerry stayed focused. "Yeah. I'm looking for her. You wouldn't know where I might find her?"

"Driver!" called Stan, and then turning his attention back to Jerry, he said, "I have no idea. But it never hurts to try calling the city morgue." The window quickly slid shut. The limousine's engine revved, and the black luxury vehicle backed up into the oncoming traffic. A passing car slammed on its brakes and triggered a domino effect of screeching brakes and honking horns. The limo then took the opportunity to navigate around Jerry's out of gas car. It rammed into the left rear of the economy rental and shoved it to the side. It backed up again and then, once clear of the tiny car, drove away at full speed down the breakdown lane. Jerry watched as it took its first right off the congested main road and disappeared from view.

"Shit," Jerry said, surveying the scene. "How am I going to deal with my luggage?" Jerry grumbled as he hoisted the gigantic (no, really, it was huge) duffel bag over his shoulder. "Friggin' Gino. Why'd he have to sell me this piece of crap? A flamethrower? How am I supposed to haul this thing around and not draw attention to myself?"

Moments after the accident and before the police (who were too busy fighting crime over at the RNC) could arrive, a taxi cab that had been stuck in the middle of the stop and go traffic, offered to give Jerry a ride. Of course, the only place he could think of to go was Jocelyn's hotel. So with horns honking and brakes again screeching, the taxi squeaked around Jerry's damaged car and over to the breakdown lane. The driver hopped out and offered to help Jerry get his luggage out of the car. The two of them slid the oversized bag across the back seat of the cab, leaving Jerry to sit in the front and stare at the meter.

Finally, they reached Jocelyn's hotel. The same front desk receptionist that Jerry had met earlier was still there.

"Did you find her?" the reception manager asked.

Thinking fast, Jerry replied, "Yeah, she's still there, but she'll be back. She wanted me to bring this stuff to her room for her."

"Well. I can take it and hold it back here for her if you

like."

Thinking faster because he had not anticipated that response, he said, "Dude. This is a family emergency! Why do you think I'm hauling around this thing? It's far too valuable to just leave behind the desk."

"Well, behind the desk is safer than in the room."

"Not if I'm in the room with it." He plunked five hundred dollars cash down on the counter. Jerry was given a key to Jocelyn's room.

With anxious curiosity, Jerry and his six-foot duffel bag quietly angled themselves and entered Jocelyn's hotel room. He could smell her perfume as he glanced around the space. Man, this woman was neat.

Everything was very tidy. Dresses hanging in the open closet. An open carry-on luggage with folded clothes was resting on the luggage rack. Shoes were lined up under it. A black leather, executive-style courier bag with an 'I support Ray Pierce" sticker stuck to it was nestled next to the shoes.

He peeked into the bathroom. Her makeup, in a Ziplock sandwich bag, and her toothbrush were on the counter.

Carefully placing the duffel bag down next to the bed, he studied himself in the large mirror hanging on the wall. Wondering what Jocelyn would think of him if she knew he was here in her room, he looked down at the little desk under the mirror and saw that Jocelyn had brought her laptop. Perfect. He whipped open the lid of the thing and... *Yes!* She was still connected to the Internet. He knew the front desk would be changing the password at midnight. He looked at his watch. Hopefully, that would be enough time.

He took the memory stick with all of Brucker's files out of his pocket and started uploading.

CHAPTER FORTY-FOUR

THE BARNACLE WAS GONE, and Jocelyn was waiting for someone to come bail her out. She had peeled off the nylons and told the policeman on duty to just throw them out hours ago when he confiscated them along with her gloves for her own protection. She had been left with the shoes, but those were pretty useless at this point. She could hardly slide her foot into the things without the nylons. The cute, little, black, pint-sized purse that she had had since the Junior Prom and the magnificent hat were missing. Both a casualty of the mass arrest at the RNC. It was just her and the little black dress now.

She was pacing around bare-legged wondering if Ethan had been able to find Sam Ballentine's phone number. Sam would get her out of here. It was just a matter of time. But time was running out. She only had twenty hours left before they would be moving her to a real jail. Not that she preferred this holding tank, but she really didn't want to get lost in some federal prison situation. According to the first policeman she asked, since she got picked up at the RNC and since that's technically the Secret Service's domain, that's where they would send her—a Federal Prison. It sounded like it might be debatable, though, because the next two policemen she asked had different answers.

Anyhow, back when she had found out that she had gotten elected to go, Samantha had been quick to congratulate her and offer her a law firm's phone number.

"Here. I have activist arrest insurance."

"Huh? What's that?" Jocelyn had asked. Sam had riffled through her purse, and that's when Jocelyn spotted a Lamar

Outdoor Advertising card sitting on Sam's desk. "Oh, Lamar. They do the billboards on Route 95..."

"I know," Sam winked as she continued to root around for the activist arrest insurance card. Jocelyn grinned. She should have guessed it! It had been Sam that put up that billboard. Sam produced a business card and showed it to Jocelyn. "It's like an insurance policy. You pay your bill to these lawyers, and anytime you get arrested, you call this number." Sam underlined the number with her finger. "They specialize in springing people who have been arrested at protests."

At first, Jocelyn had thought it was a joke. *Like, who protests that much and would recognize the cost benefit?* After Sam explained the costs of going to jail and getting out of jail, especially if you had to go to court, it did sound like a good investment.

But she hadn't called that law firm. She didn't consider herself an activist. She was just a normal person. An American. A mom. An artist. She had even claimed as such on her tax returns for a few years. Granted, she hadn't picked up a brush in years...

Anyway, as she sat in jail twiddling her thumbs, she figured she could probably write a doctoral thesis about her hypothesis that art and activism must somehow overlap. Currently, however, she was more concerned about getting some clean clothes.

"Hey, Miss America! You've got a visitor!"

Jocelyn sprung up, excited to finally be set free. She had to admit, she was more than surprised and mostly confused to see the person who was rounding the corner.

"Stojanka?"

Yup. It was Heartbreaker. She was wearing a funky sundress and a wicked cool pair of Kobi Levi shoes. Jocelyn had never seen anything like them before. Although she was curious to know why Stojanka, of all people, was there to see her, she was more curious about the shoes.

After they had covered, in depth, the origins of the footwear, Jocelyn, who was looking less than fabulous, asked Stojanka why she was there.

"Are you here to bail me out?" Jocelyn asked hopefully.

"No."

"Oh. Okay. Then why are you here?"

"I am waiting for you. I am needing to know you really here."

"Oh." Jocelyn was unable to hide her disappointment. "Yeah. I'm here. I'm not sure when I'm getting out."

"I have for you a brownie."

"Seriously?"

"Yes. I needed sweet for myself. I would share."

"Wow. Thanks!" Jocelyn looked around and wondered aloud if she was prohibited from accepting brownies.

"If you eat now. There is no evidence."

"Good point." Jocelyn gratefully gobbled up the brownie. "Thanks."

Heartbreaker made the sign of the cross and said, "May heavenly father guide you on your journey and bring you back to sit on his lap."

Jocelyn almost laughed but then figured it was some sort of translation issue.

"Goodbye," Heartbreaker said.

"Wait. You're leaving? Already? But you just got here."

"I find out what I need to know. And I know nothing."

Wow, this language barrier was pretty dense today. Not like the last time they spoke.

"Oh. Okay. Thanks for the brownie."

They said their goodbyes and Heartbreaker left.

On her way out of the police station, Heartbreaker tossed her half of the brownie into a waste basket, but she kept the pink bakery bag. Once outside, she made herself comfortable on the long granite front steps and began tearing the bag into thin strips. She was very careful with the pieces she had torn and expertly knotted them together, making two identical long lengths of pink waxed paper.

Wiping her fingers of any remnants of the brownie, she wandered over to the lamp post next to the entry of the station. A man was walking by and she coyly smiled at him as she adjusted the strap on her sundress. He raised his eyebrows and nodded on his way into the station. Once he was inside, she nonchalantly, like she did it all the time and was supposed to be there, tied one of the thin pink strips to the lamp. Then she walked over to the little maple tree across the street and tied the other strip to it.

She wouldn't have had to do this if the flags were hung on poles. Instead they were stuck to the building a-la-9/11 style because of the renovation that was supposed to be done by time the convention started. But she could handle it.

When Heartbreaker got back to her perch on the third floor of the Bank of America building across the street and to the right of the entrance of the station, she looked through her Schmidt & Bender scope. Sure, it was expensive, but damn, did it blow that Carl Zeiss thing away. She loved her new Schmidt & Bender! Loved it. It was the perfect complement for her Custom Accuracy International .260 Remington. She could see those pink strips of paper as clear as day, and they would definitely help her figure her windage. This was going to be so simple. Now all she had to do was hurry up and wait.

CHAPTER FORTY-FIVE

Basel, Switzerland

"I SHOULD LET YOU KNOW, Mr. Lowe, that I am in receipt of the book you had shipped to me," Jonas Ledergerber commented as he slowly turned away from the window. He was, as per usual, wearing a perfect suit, and Ethan wondered if the man made a special point of standing in order to showcase his attire. "General Vaughn has expressed his appreciation. I was happy to help him. For now, he shall help me." Ledergerber assumed a classic Jesus Christ pose, a gesture with both hands gently outstretched. "After all, we are all in this together. Are we not?"

Ethan rolled his eyes, amazed that this guy took himself seriously. "Oh, you mean the book that *I* sent you? What makes that book so special anyway? It's not very well written," he commented as he entered the office and the double doors closed silently behind him. The office, despite the sun pouring through the windows, was cool, smelled like an expensive hotel, and offered a luxury that only real money can afford—complete and total privacy.

"Ah, so you looked at it." Ledergerber looked pleased. "Did you recognize anyone in the photographs?" Ethan blandly shook his head 'no,' and the suited man motioned for him to come closer as he casually strode over to his desk and produced the red hardbound book. Ledergerber sat down, placed the book squarely in front of him, and began delicately flipping the pages. "This one," he pronounced as he pointed to the photo.

Ethan spun the book around to look at the black and white image of two men, shaking hands, flanked by smiling children. "That's General Vaughn. Makes sense since the book is about military contracting. Who's he with?"

"Why, yes, this is from his meeting with Slobodan Milošević, the U.S. enemy in Kosovo at the time." Ethan tightened his brow because he had worked for Vaughn's mercenary division while at the Conglomerate. "But that should not be of concern to you. The two had contracts," Ledergerber continued. "The children. You perhaps recognize someone, no?"

Ethan scanned the picture, and his eyes instantly jolted to a halt at the likeness of a young Heartbreaker. The Heartbreaker he remembered was tucked in between more than a dozen other happy children. He breathed deeply through his nose and replied simply, "No" and pushed the book back to Ledergerber.

Ledergerber accepted the book and smoothed the page carefully with his well-manicured hand. "All those children, so sweet," he sighed. "They were paid to be there. Makes for a nice photo, don't you think?"

Still standing at the desk, Ethan nodded. "Yup. Real Pulitzer Prize material."

Ledergerber chuckled. "Yes. It is better that the picture not be in circulation at present. One of those young girls is now grown and currently under contract." He shut the book with a deliberate finality and faced Ethan. "I have also listened to the interview with your woman, Jocelyn. Very interesting."

"She's innocent, Ledergerber. She doesn't know anything," Ethan remarked, casually while reaching over the desk to collect his payment for the enhanced interrogation job. He felt a sickening in his stomach taking the money. He was almost certain that this whole visit was a setup. The job he had been tasked with was way too easy, to the point of unnecessary, and now this thing with Heartbreaker, one of the most precise and talented shooters he'd ever encountered in real life...

"I am more interested in why you felt the need to send me a recording of that conversation with your woman, Mr. Lowe."

The statement took Ethan off guard, and he didn't know how to answer. So he didn't. He just kept his eyes locked with Ledergerber's probing gaze for longer than necessary and then changed the topic.

"What's the deal with the friggin' butterfly pins?" Ethan asked as he flipped through the money in the envelope. "I ran across another one during this last job. Is there a reason why they keep cropping up?"

Jonas Ledergerber raised his eyebrow and smiled. "There are less than you imagine, Mr. Lowe. Delohim has produced and donated thirty-three of them. The proceeds from the jewelry are being funneled to a politician in the United States who has worked very hard. It is our agreement."

"Who?" Ethan asked as he took a seat opposite the desk. "The president for his re-election?" He had no love for the current president and honestly would not be surprised if part of his enormous one-billion-dollar re-election fund was bankrolled by these stupid pins.

"No. The ball has to be served from the other side of the court now."

"Oh, you mean Rooney?"

Ledergerber laughed and extinguished a cigarette that had been sitting in his ashtray. Ethan had noticed that this guy had a habit of lighting up a cigarette, taking one or two puffs, then ignoring the thing until he finally just snubbed it out.

The Swiss gentleman continued, "It is no secret that our associate, billionaire Peter Thiel, founder of PayPal, has given more than two and a half million dollars in staggered amounts to the Raymond Pierce campaign. In fact, he announced the agreement to the world when he summoned your American television show <u>*Sixty Minutes*</u> to conduct an interview. You might remember that it was *after* Pierce was obviously no longer a contender for President of the United States that the agreement had been publicized." He paused and eyed Ethan. "Don't you think it odd that Thiel continued to donate money *after* Dr. Pierce had officially no chance of becoming president? When the campaign was officially declared over?"

Ethan was intrigued, mostly because of Jocelyn's unhealthy obsession with Ray Pierce. Thiel, he knew, was a member of the Bilderberg Group's Steering Committee, and they were always an interesting crowd. Nothing would surprise him if they were involved. "You mean they have been paying Pierce to take a fall?" he asked, while making himself comfortable in the arm chair opposite Ledergerber.

"Not exactly, Mr. Lowe. The system itself is falling, and a new one is emerging. We are compensating Dr. Pierce for his time, and he has made the wise decision to accept. He has been an invaluable gatekeeper." Ledergerber gazed out the wall of a window down onto the city of Basel and continued, "Ultimately, the death of the U.S. dollar will be applauded in the mainstream media as a necessary and good thing. It will be marketed as 'karma' and they will call it 'progress.' They will even call it 'decentralization' and a success for the free market." He folded his hands on the desk and watched Ethan as he spoke. "But it will not feel like a beneficial development for the people who will suffer greatly as the dollar dies. The people will not know what has struck them as they can only conceptualize this type of devastation being inflicted by munitions. Therefore, violence and wars will, of course, develop, providing ample cover for the spread of this new system. Only those educated in the underpinnings of shadow banking will understand the whole thing as a charade designed to hide the complete centralization of sovereign economic governance into the hands of the globalists. The International Monetary Fund and Bank of International Settlements will be hailed as 'fiscal heroes,' saving the world from a state of economic destruction that the elites themselves created."

Ethan grunted. "Oh, so you're saying American

citizenship is a front row ticket to the freak show?" Ledergerber let out a blue-blooded type of snort and chuckled. "Figures," Ethan grumbled, as he toyed with a Meisterstück Classique Montblanc pen that had been sitting on the little table next to his chair. This was the most excited Ethan had seen this man. Then again, this was the first time Ethan had gotten himself in the game and bothered to actually listen to him, considering that his distrust for the man was growing by the minute.

Ledergerber leaned forward and, uncharacteristically, seemed to really want to communicate with Ethan. "It will be under the Ray Pierce banner that others will introduce the new system. They will use the same verbiage as Dr. Pierce, but because there is no way for the collective of the United States of America to effectively engage in debate about banking, where banking policy and history intersect, and usury..." He made an arbitrary flourish with his hand. "Let alone about who owns the Federal Reserve, creating money out of the ether, and fractional reserve banking. Well, this is, by design, too much for the average American to process. Their money is like water to them, the unnoticed vital life force that animates them. Do you think the guardians of this powerful flow of energy care about what it is called or which country claims ownership? Hardly." Ethan watched as Ledergerber sat erect in his chair, raised his chin and made an audible, aristocratic sniff before continuing.

"Dr. Pierce has grown the ranks of the Republican Party in the United States. This is important. He has done for the Republicans what the president has done for American Democrats. What good would it be for us if the American public did not believe in the system we have created?"

"Fuck the system," Ethan balked and twirled the pen in his fingers.

Ledergerber smiled broadly. "Tell me. What would happen if the general public stopped believing that it was their votes that had wrought such misfortune? If they did not believe they could vote the problem away? Where would they turn their ire if they weren't blaming each other?" He stopped to let that sink in and slid a fresh cigarette from the wooden cigarette box on his desk.

"Dr. Pierce has done an exquisite job," he said, tapping the cigarette on the table. "He has helped prime the Americans for the eventuality of the new system while embedding a renewed interest in preserving the political structure. He is a powerful global brand. The brand that he has created will be leveraged and co-opted. It has already started. It will serve us well moving forward. He deserves his reward."

Ethan studied Ledergerber lighting his next cigarette. "*Pardonnez-moi*," Ledergerber apologized. "Would you care for one?" He held out the lit cigarette, offering it to Ethan. Ethan shook his head. "Very well then," he sighed. "Such a shame I cannot even enjoy a cigarette with you before you must depart." The way Ledergerber said 'depart' made the hairs on the back of Ethan's neck bristle. *Dearly departed.* He couldn't shake off the funeral connection his mind was drumming up. "Have we discussed HUD yet? You and I?" Ledergerber asked using the lit cigarette to point back and forth between the two of them.

When Ethan indicated that they had not, Ledergerber began his spiel about dark money, covert operation budgets, and the whole scene with shadow banking and mortgages. Ethan let him ramble on until he heard Ledergerber utter the words, 'This is God's work,' and that was it.

"Depends which god you're worshiping," Ethan remarked as he pushed himself out of the chair and casually extended himself over the modern art-inspired desk to shake hands. Ledergerber raised a thin brow, smiled and extended his hand. But instead of a firm handshake, Ethan instantly grabbed Ledergerber above the wrist and yanked him over the desk while jamming the ridiculously expensive pen directly into the Swiss gentleman's larynx. As blood silently dribbled onto the desk and soiled the fine white collar, Jonas Ledergerber's ability to speak or scream disappeared. Ethan, emotionless, watched the man struggle and weakly fade away. He wondered how on earth he had ever allowed this pencil-neck of a man to assume any sort of dominance over him in the first place as he jerked the pen out of Ledergerber's throat.

Thinking fast but moving slowly, he fished a hundred dollar bill out of his jacket, wiped down the bloody pen with the bill and placed both the pen and the money under Ledergerber's still limp hand. He studied the scene for a moment, then took all the money in the manila envelope and threw it at Ledergerber. Federal Reserve notes fluttered down around the blood-stained, lifeless suit as Ethan showed himself the door.

CHAPTER FORTY-SIX

Meanwhile
Providence, Rhode Island

"WHAT THE HELL?" FBI Special Agent Dobson sighed as he hung up the phone. Reams and reams of paper were spitting out of the FBI branch office's Ricoh 3100-sheet capacity printer. At first, he had thought it was some sort of typical malfunction with the photocopier, and he went to shut the thing off. "Figures. Closing time and this has to happen," Dobson grumbled as he repeatedly pushed the big red stop button.

But it wouldn't shut off. It just kept going and going like a crack-addled Energizer bunny. Dobson was really miffed, but then perplexed when he started gathering up the papers that were flying all over the place.

"Holy shit," he whispered as he studied what he was holding.

McDonnell wandered in holding his coat and car keys and saw the mess. "Christ, man, what did you do to the copier?" Dobson, still holding a haphazard pile of paper, made eye contact with McDonnell and shook his head in despair as more paper flew toward him, bounced off his thigh and onto the floor. With the mechanized sound of the copier providing almost musical accompaniment, McDonnell walked over to the machine and pulled the plug out of the wall. However, much to his dismay, the machine kept churning out documents.

"Backup battery," Dobson explained while still collecting paper.

"Well, it's gotta run out of paper soon. Right?"

McDonnell offered, hopefully.

"I guess. But just help me pick this stuff up. We gotta burn this shit."

"Huh?"

"Buddy, we're fucked. Just help me pick this all up. Now!"

McDonnell did as he was told and started picking up random sheets of paper. "What's going on?" McDonnell wanted to know. Then, when he noticed what he was holding, namely documentation of his dealings with Robert King, he started trembling. "Aw, fuck. Where's this coming from?"

Dobson opened his bottom desk drawer, removed his emergency flask, took a gulp and handed it to McDonnell. The papers were still flying out of the machine, and they were both scared shitless. The stuff the copier was vomiting was all sorts of incriminating. Obviously, they would lose their jobs, stand trial, and probably be forced to testify against someone who was likely to kill them or their families.

"Where is this coming from?!" McDonnell demanded.

Eventually, later that night, Dobson, the more technically literate of the pair, figured out that the dump of digital secrets was originating from Tampa, Florida. In a fit of drunken inspiration, they decided to fly to Tampa, sling their FBI badass-ness around, and contain the situation, if that was at all possible.

"Witness protection program, here we come!" they toasted in solidarity as they shot down some Jack Daniel's at the airport. They, especially McDonnell, knew they were expendable and figured it was only a matter of time.

CHAPTER FORTY-SEVEN

The next morning
Tampa, Florida

"OKAY, SWEETHEART. IT'S TIME."

Jocelyn couldn't believe it. No one had come for her. It wasn't like she had anything to gather up. She stood up and prepared to walk barefoot out of the cell. "This is the definition of pathetic," she grumbled, and then asked, "Can I at least make one more call and leave a message for someone? To let them know that I'm going someplace else."

Jocelyn was now really worried about the kids. The police guards, she thought, were beginning to feel bad for her. She had harassed them interminably last night, and they finally broke down and let her try calling again. Unfortunately, she had dialed the wrong number.

"Really? You don't know your own mother's number?"

"Well, it's in my cell phone, and I never actually dial it," she said while hurriedly attempting another number.

"What kind of daughter are you?"

At the time, Jocelyn hadn't been sure if that was joke or not. Now she was considering the question very seriously.

"Nope. You got your shot last night," the officer said as he ushered her out of the cell.

Last night had been pretty horrible. After she had eaten the brownie and Heartbreaker left, she thought she was going to snap listening to the nonstop talk radio that the guard seemed to be enjoying. Eventually, after some gentle haranguing, the guard changed it to an oldies station, which consisted of a wide-sweeping melange of '70s and '80s pop songs.

Being very uncomfortable on the bench/cot, she had started with the ultimately futile phone call requests. At that point, she was grateful that at least she wasn't listening to talk radio. But something funny started to happen. The songs had started to talk to her. Directly to her. She had recognized the familiar Pop-y, Reggae stylings of a GDAE bass line. One of the songs she remembered from Junior High School was taking on monumental significance.

There is no political solution...
There is no bloody revolution...
With words they try to jail ya...

Then, after listening to *'Girls Just Wanna Have Fun'*, she decided that the songs really weren't talking to her, and she asked the guard to just shut off the whole thing, or at least turn it down so that she could get some sleep. Unfortunately for her, when she finally did fall asleep, it was just a mess of nightmares. Ethan was shooting her again. The kids were crying. Her gorgeous black hat had grown legs and was walking around all by itself.

Needless to say, by morning she was exhausted. She had not eaten anything that was on her prescribed diet. She had not had any of her supplements or remedies that her homeopath had given her, and she had a horrible stomach ache. She wasn't sure if her malaise was because she was starting to get seriously depressed about the useless folly of her whole 'performance art' project or because she was actually starting to experience another M.S. exacerbation. But she was weak. Really weak.

"I'm sorry, sweetheart, but I have to do this during transport. I'll give you the option of front or back. Your choice."

Jocelyn was confused until she saw the zip-ties. "Sorta

like me asking my kids if they want a red or blue sweater." She was unhappily compliant as the officer zipped her wrists together in front of her. She glanced up, and that's when she saw him walking around the corner with... *no way!* He had her black hat in his hand. "Ethan?"

Her legs gave out, and she collapsed.

Ethan dropped the hat and ran over to help her up. "Jesus, Joss. Look at you. What happened?" he said, kneeling next to her, helping her sit up.

The policeman who had zip-tied her wrists hurriedly cut off the restraints. Ethan smoothed her hair to the side of her face, and the officer returned holding a little cup of water. Ethan took it and held it until Jocelyn was ready to hold it herself.

"What happened to you?" she asked.

"What happened to *you*?" he corrected.

"Ethan," she whimpered, "how come I've been in here for so long?"

Instantly, and Jocelyn should have seen this coming because it was so typical, Ethan went on the defensive. "Oh, for Christ's sake, Joss! I mean, I was in Europe! What was I supposed to do? I couldn't find your friend Samantha's number, and it's not my fault that you're all messed up in jail. I just spent a ton of money to be here right now. So, seriously, lay off, all right! You should be thanking me!"

Of course, Jocelyn was in no mood to debate the fact that he had agreed to take care of the kids while she was away. Nor was it worth it to point out the obvious—that if he was feeling short on money, then how the heck was he getting back and forth to Europe lately? Instead, she just took a sip of water and said, "Thank you, Ethan. Thank you for being here. They were getting ready to transport me to a federal prison. You got here just in time."

He looked at her as if she was somehow making fun of him by saying this. He left her there to sip her water as he dealt with the bailout. Naturally, he only had Euros on him, and she heard the policeman say, “Are you kidding me? You got a credit card or something?” Of course, he did. Why he felt compelled to demonstrate that he had actually been in Europe when he had a credit card all along was just irritating Jocelyn even more.

She stood up. Gathered her shoes and put them on. Then she picked up the hat and plunked it on her head. She was trying to figure out how they would get back to her hotel so that she could take a much-needed shower and change. On the way, she wanted to borrow Ethan’s phone and call the kids. Man, she missed them.

CHAPTER FORTY-EIGHT

Meanwhile

JERRY WAS HIKING up the street with his enormous duffel bag. It was pretty amazing that he had gotten this close to the police station with this thing. He had taken the bus and followed the guy at the reception desk's directions to find the police station nearest the convention center. Stan's comment about calling the morgue had really freaked him out. He figured he'd start with the police and see if she was, you know, still alive and all. They'd know where the morgue was in any event. She hadn't come back to the hotel last night, and he was worried.

Now that the RNC was officially over, the city was basically back to normal. People didn't have to walk through fenced in sidewalks or follow a path outlined in Jersey barriers. There were no random credential checks. Perhaps it was because it didn't even look like a gun, or maybe, because it was technically totally legal, no one seemed to give a hoot. Not that anyone even looked in Jerry's general direction anyway.

Jerry, however, was very conscious of what he was carrying. He didn't want to bring it into the police station with him. He wanted to go inside. Just to check. As he pondered how to deal with the duffle bag situation, he stopped in his tracks. A white Chevy Impala had just pulled up, rather haphazardly, in front of the police station. Two men in really wrinkly suits got out. Jerry couldn't help but watch them as they bumbled all over themselves.

"McDonnell! Buddy! It's over here!" One of the suited

guys was shouting to the other suit who was staggering off in the opposite direction.

"This is a frucking nightmare," McDonnell slurred. "Here. Sponge Bob. Dobson. Whatever your name is! Just take my muuutherfrrrucking gun," McDonnell blurted while unsteadily holding his gun out for his partner. "Just shoot me! Kill me right now!" He paused and very solemnly announced, "I can take it. I can take it like a man."

"Okay. Okay, *just relax." Dobson helped McDonnell gain his footing and supported him while steering him back to* the Impala.

McDonnell continued, "Like a *real* muufrerkukkin man."

"I know. I know. A real man," Jerry heard the other guy, Dobson say. Jerry noted that Dobson appeared fairly drunk himself, but nowhere near as impaired as his partner. Dobson opened the car door and tried to coax McDonnell to just sit and relax.

"I'm driving! The man always drives!"

As Jerry watched the goings-on, he marveled that it was all happening right in front of the police station. He decided that he had better give these guys a wide berth. Or better yet, just hang back until they had figured out what they were doing. He retreated across the street to a park bench to watch the action.

Meanwhile, Heartbreaker was watching with curious interest through her new scope, but she was concerned. She knew the scope was good. Really good. But she could have sworn that she saw the Colonel go into the station a little while ago. Of course, she hadn't seen him for some time now... And what were those drunk guys doing? Some sort of distraction action? She convinced herself that she was just tired, and she pinched her wrist until it cried red. She'd wait.

CHAPTER FORTY-NINE

ETHAN FINISHED THE POLICE PAPERWORK, and Jocelyn just had to sign a couple of things.

"Thank you," she said again as she hugged him for coming to her rescue. Then she shouldn't have said it, but she did: "Did you put on weight? You feel... you feel thicker or something."

"Well, maybe you got skinnier or something."

"I probably did. This whole trip has been a disaster," she sighed.

"I could have told you that, Joss," he grumbled as they made their way through the newly renovated station—lots of new glass walls and slippery tiled floors. The place even smelled new, or at least really clean compared to the cell she had been locked up in. Her fancy, too-high wedge shoes without stockings were painful, and she grimaced as Ethan spoke.

"The RNC," he spat. "Like, who came up with this whole convoluted party thing? Whose great idea was it that I should take time out of my life to vote for someone who was going to tell me what to do? Why would anyone think that was a good idea?" He held the door for her and she held her hat to her head as they turned into the long hallway which led to the exit.

He continued with his polemic. "Soon, very soon, Jocelyn, everyone is going to see the two D.C. based political parties for what they really are. One big cluster fuck of thieves that have effectively destroyed this country. Those assholes are all owned by someone, Joss. The money... the fucking money that was spent to get them there and... the money... "

As Ethan trailed off, Jocelyn thought about the money she had spent to get herself here and hobbled to catch up with him. The shoes were torture. He slowed down and continued a bit more thoughtfully. "The laws they pass will lose all legitimacy with the voting public when nice people like *you* finally refuse to participate in their game. A game where they make the rules, change the rules mid-play, and if they lose, claim that the rules were never meant for them in the first place." He shook his head. "Oh, and as an added benefit, staying away from the whole game means that your good name will not be tarnished by association when the shit really does start hitting the fan."

"But Ethan—" she interrupted, and he kept talking.

"Do me a favor, Joss. Don't associate with them. Any of them," he said with pointed disdain. "And by 'them,' I mean anything that even smells political, and I don't care if it's called a 'party' or a 'movement' or whatever. You can still help solve the problems of the world, but do it directly yourself. Volunteer at a soup kitchen or something. Shit, you've been volunteering for Ray Pierce for a really long time now. Help a real-life person in need right in your neighborhood, not some grandiose, sweeping political campaign. Keep things simple. Okay? This kills me to see you going through all this for this guy, Joss. It's just not worth it." He stopped walking and turned to face her. She stopped and met his gaze as he continued.

"Look, only one percent of Occupy Wall Street's famous 'one percent' completely control the outcome of the election, and they own everyone." Ethan had started using his hands for emphasis. "That's a club of thirty-two thousand people out of well over *three hundred million* Americans. And that's just the documented donations from this group." Jocelyn fought back a bunch of emotions. She really didn't feel like debating or arguing with him. She just wanted to go home.

"But Ethan—"

"Let me finish!" He grabbed her by the shoulders. "It's a

moral decision, Joss. It's a moral decision to quit the game and denounce it for the obvious bullshit fraud it is. Don't settle and compromise yourself for a system that you know is corrupt in hopes of somehow 'taking *them* over' and converting '*them*' to the forces of good. You have about the same chance of infiltrating the Mafia and reforming it."

"Ethan, stop talking! I get it!" She brushed his hands away and unconsciously stomped her foot. She noticed the cameras mounted on the ceiling of the lonely hallway and tried to compose herself. "I lived it. You don't have to rub this in. Why do you think I wanted this hat?" She tapped the brim with her fingers. "What do you think it represents?" She glared at him. "I'm in mourning. I'm sad, damn it. I didn't want to believe it, and I held out hope for a long time. I wanted it to work the way that I thought it was supposed to work. Like some sort of Saturday morning School House Rock cartoon or something." She sighed and rolled her eyes. "I thought it was just that people weren't seeing beyond a marketing campaign—"

"No. *You* weren't seeing beyond a marketing campaign," he interrupted.

"Would you please let me finish? I let you talk," Jocelyn huffed, and they smirked at each other before she began again. "I thought if I could just warn them. But I have to say, you're right—especially after seeing how a political party operates. It's like one fraternity hazing after another. I've extended my energy, my intelligence, and my time all over the place. I get it. Seriously," she pointed to the hat, "what do you think this represents?"

Before Ethan could offer a guess she said, "This hat is a distress signal and," she swallowed hard, "a celebration of individual liberty. The equivalent of me marching around waving a black flag and shouting 'anarchy!' Quite frankly, at this point, I'm not even sure what the right course of action is anymore. Do a Constitutional Convention and re-write the thing? Probably. That's what it says to do right there in the document. I mean, it's in black and white." She shrugged. "But that's just another opportunity for a huge marketing campaign to roll in and sell everyone a load of goods." Ethan's eyes lit up as Jocelyn spoke and his face seemed to relax a little. "I don't know, but I tried. The system is broken, and the sad part is that it was probably designed that way in the first place. I finally figured that the only thing I could personally, effectively do was to *be* the black flag. I'm not crazy, Ethan. They are." She jabbed her index finger toward the world outside the police station.

He looked at her, and she couldn't tell for sure, but she thought she spotted some flicker of emotion in him that she hadn't seen in a long time. "Damn it, Joss..."

"What? It's true. Maybe I'll write a book about this whole experience or something."

He nodded solemnly. "Look, when we get out there, just stick near me. You're probably more dangerous than they know."

"What's that supposed to mean?"

He opened the door, but this time he didn't let her go first, he just walked out, and she followed. As Jocelyn's eyes adjusted to the natural light, little threads of pink wax paper were swaying ever so gently in the breeze, and a seemingly out of context Chevy Impala sped, in reverse, toward a fire hydrant.

"What the hell?" Ethan said.

It all happened so suddenly. Too suddenly. The car crashed into the hydrant, and like all good hydrant crashes, water flew up and all over the place like a geyser. A man in a wrinkled suit was running toward the car and getting completely saturated with geyser rain. He tore open the driver's side door shouting, "McDonnell! McDonnell, buddy!" only to expose the fact that McDonnell, seconds before, had blown his own brains out. Bloody chunks were still sliding down the driver's side window.

Little did Jocelyn and Ethan (or the police for that matter) realize, that during their anarchistic bonding session, a full on battle was fermenting out front. Drunk FBI guys had been wielding their guns at each other (one of whom had just blown his brains out), and some hapless, gun-toting retiree walking in the park across the street had decided to try and intervene.

The surviving FBI agent assumed that the concerned citizen was out to kill him and started firing ill-placed bullets. This prompted the silver-haired good Samaritan to squeeze off a few shots from his Glock 17 and run. The rest of the street, seemingly all aware of the scene at the very same moment, started screaming and running around in random directions. Jerry had already whipped out what he had been lugging around in that six-foot-long duffel bag—namely a brand new military-grade flamethrower.

Bursts of flames hissed as water spewed from the geyser and random shots rang out. Ethan grabbed Jocelyn and tried to push her back into the building. That's when a very specific bullet hit Ethan squarely in the back. He fell forward onto the ground. On the next shot, Jocelyn fell against the wall of the police station. Instantly, she felt another bullet enter her chest and felt a splash of blood across her face.

With bullets now flying almost everywhere and a random lone bush, conveniently burning for dramatic and allegorical effect, Ethan whispered through clenched teeth, "Don't move. Make her think you're dead. I won't let you die." But Jocelyn felt herself floating away.

CHAPTER FIFTY

AS THE POLICE, who had been hurriedly changing into their riot gear, emerged and squad cars came hollering back from all points, Jocelyn did what she unconsciously and habitually did in times of severe stress. She floated away. Not all the way away, just slightly to her left.

She was still conscious and was aware of the pain, but it was an altered state of consciousness. She had removed herself slightly from the whole scene and was just an observer. She knew that she had tears rolling down her face and boogers coming out of her nose and that she had lost bladder control. She knew all this, but it didn't bother her. She was just observing. For a fleeting moment, she perceived fire. It wouldn't be until the ambulance came and they put her on the stretcher that she started seeing herself from a different perspective. She was no longer on her left. She was above now. As the ambulance raced toward the emergency room and the EMTs hustled about treating her wounds, her consciousness spread even farther from its former point of assemblage.

She had a bird's eye view of the ambulance that she now appreciated was traveling in slow motion though the city. She was becoming less concerned about her body and more curious about the new perspective she had. Everything looked—no, that's the wrong word. Everything *felt* like it was a continuation of some sort of three-dimensional, gently undulating, Seurat pointillist painting.

Jocelyn marveled at how the infinity of colorful dabs were each pulling their own weight in the only way they knew how, composing this scene of blinding temporal purity. A scene that had arranged itself ever so perfectly for this very moment and just for her. All the parts were working together in many more dimensions than Jocelyn had ever appreciated before. She couldn't help but being, awed knowing that this delicate display was in constant motion. Forever and always disappearing and reappearing in an elegant Mobius Strip made of nothing and everything.

She wanted to experience more of this, but something dragged her back down closer to earth. Her change in perspective probably had something to do with the IV that the EMTs were dealing with, but she didn't care. Her expanded vision caught the image of her black hat. Her gorgeous black hat tumbling down the city street. She instantly recognized it and watched as a young Hispanic girl picked it up, studied it, and popped it on her head.

"¿De dónde sacaste ese sombrero?" the girl's pregnant mother, who was pushing a stroller and distracted by another one of her children crossing the street, asked in surprise when she saw the hat.

"Me pareció. Se me ocurrió," the child answered. It was true, she had found it, and it had just come to her.

The mother concluded that someone would be looking for such an impressive hat and told her daughter to just leave the hat where it was. "Dejarlo aquí."

The little girl, like Jocelyn had been, was wildly attracted to this hat, and in typical six-year-old form said, "No. Me pertenece. Y nadie puede quitárselo." It really did belong to her and, as the child insisted, no one could take it away.

Just before they rushed her into the operating room, Jocelyn muttered, "You go, girl. Wear it in good health. Here's to the future."

CHAPTER FIFTY-ONE

THE BEEPING IS WHAT WOKE HER UP. All sorts of disjointed beeping. Tubes and wires. They had taken her off the respirator about an hour ago, but she had taken a nap since then. Now the nurse hovering around her was asking questions and scribbling on the chart.

She was still groggy after the four-hour thoracic surgery and the requisite medically-induced coma. The only thing she really appreciated amongst the phalo green and shiny white of the Intensive Care Unit room in which she found herself was the window to the outside world. This bright spot was located opposite the wall with the window to the nurses' station. *There's nurses everywhere. That's good. Kinda creepy though,* she thought. The nurses watched her constantly.

She turned her head away from the window with all the nurses peering at her and watched the clouds floating by outside. *They look just like the clouds at the beginning of The Simpsons*, she marveled. At the thought of the cartoon series, she remembered that she had kids, and a tear rolled down her face.

"Are my babies okay?" Jocelyn asked the nurse while still looking at the clouds.

"I'm sure they're fine," the nurse remarked. Jocelyn didn't like the tone. She could tell the lady didn't know.

She doesn't know my kids. She doesn't know how sensitive William is. I'll be okay, Willy. I love you too, Lilly. She directed these thoughts to her children as she stared at the clouds. She was so overwhelmed with love for both of them. She remembered the day they were born and welled up. That was the last, and only, time she ever remembered being in a hospital. Ethan had been there with her for their birth. *Oh, my*

God! Ethan!

Jocelyn struggled to turn her head toward the nurse. “Is Ethan okay? He got shot.”

Just then, before the nurse could answer, a man entered the room. Her vision poured over the Gentleman’s Warehouse suit. She didn’t recognize this person.

“Oh. Hello.” She blinked and watched the nurse nod at the man.

The suit cautiously approached her bed. She was focused, for some reason, on noticing the man’s hands unbuttoning the suit jacket as the monotonous, overlapping beeps and buzzes drilled slowly, like Chinese water torture, into her head.

“Hello, Ms. McLaren. I’m Special Agent Mark Witherall,” he announced as he produced his FBI credentials.

“Who isn’t special?” Jocelyn asked, attempting a joke. Almost instantly, she realized that the joke wasn’t funny, and she scrunched her nose, displeased with herself for even saying it. Of course, this only made her look as stoned as she felt.

S.A. Witherall studied her as he put away his identification. “You’ve been messed up with some heavy stuff, huh?” Jocelyn wasn’t sure if he was talking about the morphine that was coursing through her veins via the little tube taped to her hand or if he was addressing the fact that she just had two bullets removed from her body.

“I guess,” she feebly responded.

“Do you recognize this?” Witherall asked as he held up a piece of paper which read:

⇉ ↳↺ ⌃⇇⇅ ⇵⇇↶⍲⌃ ⇉↪ ⌃⇇⇅ ↺↳⇁⇇
⇉↪⇅
↳↪⇆
⇉ ↙↕◁⇨ ◢↕▶

Confused, Jocelyn started chuckling. “Did it come from a UFO?”

"No. It came from your laptop," he said, placing the paper on her over-the-bed table.

"Huh?" She stopped giggling. It hurt to laugh anyway.

"Look, S.A... What did you say your name was?"

"Witherall. Mark Witherall."

"I wouldn't recognize my own name right now, I'm so loopy. Is this some sort of test or something?"

"That's what we're trying to figure out," Witherall replied. Jocelyn noticed the nurse tilting her head to look at the paper. "This message, along with over sixteen *thousand* pages, was blasted across the entire FBI network." He paused and added, "Via the photocopiers. There was a lot of paper involved. So much for that 'Think Green - save a tree' initiative," Witherall said without cracking a smile. Jocelyn closed her eyes and tried to wake up from the dream, but it wasn't a dream. "Every FBI office in the United States now has a bunch of information about Formula One race cars, a portfolio of Carlos Delohim jewelry, as well as a nice stash of child pornography. Fascinating stuff."

The metronome that was Jocelyn's heart monitor started to beep a little quicker.

"My computer did this? I honestly don't know..."

"Fortunately, we do. One of the Rhode Island agents you had been in contact with was recently arrested. His partner suffered a self-inflicted gunshot wound to the right temple. He's dead. They both worked, at one point, for the child pornography unit. And according to the messages we received from your computer, they were scooping up images, trading them for favors and information, while intimidating or eliminating the competition of the original publishers by arresting them and shutting down their sites. They then published the porn themselves. A little side job, I guess." Again, he paused and watched her. "They had been rerouting images being sent to someone you used to work with."

"Robert King," she sighed.

"So you know about this?"

"No. Yes. But I was too busy increasing shareholder value. I mean, I didn't know until Jerry figured it out. We thought the porn was some sort of terrorist code at first."

The FBI agent shook his head. "No. That would have been the emails that were being propagated through your division's server. They were cleverly disguised as junk mail—spam. That's what I was working on—the spam stuff. I'm actually in the cyber-security unit," he said while jamming his hands in his pockets. "Apparently, quite a few different alphabet agencies are interested in the goings-on at your former place of employment. Even INTERPOL is now involved with the files regarding a wine import/export business, and they are more than curious about the McLaren Racing stuff." Her brain felt so fluffy that she thought that she might either float away or vomit. The metronome was beating faster. "Jocelyn, Jerry doesn't happen to be the same man that the Tampa P.D. arrested for burning down a bench and destroying some bushes with a flamethrower the day you were shot, does it?"

Jocelyn, because of the pain, was clutching her chest, and her heart monitor was beeping all over the place. "Jerry?" Other tones connected to her vitals were going off now, too. The nurse was pressing buttons, and Special Agent What's-His-Name was eyeing her closely as she finally sputtered, "A flamethrower? I'm sorry, but I think I'm too wasted to really understand what's going on here."

"Jerry Apario said in his statement that he arrived at the police station to bail *you* out, and upon seeing you get shot—and this is according to him—he assembled the flamethrower for personal protection and it got out of hand." Both the nurse and Jocelyn looked at Witherall in complete disbelief.

"What the..? Who walks around with a flamethrower?" the nurse remarked, and Jocelyn broke into laughter, which quickly devolved into painful moaning.

The nurse looked at Witherall and shook her head. "She's not ready for this. We've been keeping her unconscious for the past twenty-nine hours while she was on the respirator. I'm going to have to ask you to leave."

"No." Jocelyn's hand, tethered to the IV, shot out. "No. Don't leave." Both the nurse and Witherall looked at Jocelyn. "This is crazy. I need to know what the heck is going on."

"So do we," Witherall said, not so much to Jocelyn but to the nurse.

The nurse, still looking at the monitors, shook her head. Turning to Jocelyn, she said, "You really should rest. You've been through a lot. By the looks of it, you aren't going anywhere soon. You have tubes draining the fluid from your lungs right now, and we want to take those out in a little while. I can have him come back another day."

"No. Please. Just tell me. Jerry had a flamethrower?"

"Yes. A brand new model." He shook his head. "Interestingly enough, during questioning, he gave the police a beeper and told them he would turn state's evidence regarding mafia activity in Rhode Island if he could be placed in the witness protection program."

"Oh, he would like that." Jocelyn smiled dreamily. "He always wanted to be a ghost." Witherall seemed to freeze at that statement, and Jocelyn continued. "Is Ethan okay? I think he got shot, too. Did he get burned by the flamethrower?" Then, recalling her patchwork memory of the event asked, "I'm not burned, am I?"

"No. Neither one of you got burnt. He's fine."

"He is?"

"Yes. Apparently, he was wearing a fairly advanced bullet proof vest."

"Oh," she said with a faraway look. "That's why he felt so thick when I hugged him..." Her voice trailed off as she tried to recall the last time she saw him. They were talking about politics. In a police station. "So he knew we were going to get shot at?"

"The police and the FBI have questioned him rather thoroughly about that, and he hasn't offered any information other than he maintains that he has a right, which he does, to wear body armor."

"Oh." The quiet cacophony of disjointed beeping was settling down, and no one spoke.

Finally, when her heart rate was somewhere close to normal, Witherhall asked, "Jocelyn, do you know a man named Timothy Brucker?" The beeping kicked up a notch. Jocelyn quickly arrived at the conclusion that trying to lie with a heart monitor strapped to you, while on serious pain meds, was pretty much futile.

"I know this person. Yes. He visited me the day his car blew up." Jocelyn thought she heard the nurse mutter, 'Oh, for the love of God.'

Witherall nodded. "It looks as if all these papers that the FBI got were originally the property of Mister Brucker. We are still piecing this all together, but it appears Brucker knew he was going to get killed. He was a blackmailer extraordinaire, and one of the entities he was attempting to extort called his bluff and murdered him."

"I don't understand. Brucker's been dead for months now, right? Why did I get shot? Who the heck shot me?" she whined.

"We don't know. There are a bunch of references to a lawsuit involving McLaren Racing Company. We need you to help us help you. "

"Oh. I get it. You're from the government, and you're here to help." Jocelyn closed her eyes and carefully positioned her head back onto the pillows. Suddenly, her mouth was extremely dry and she asked the nurse for some water. The nurse magically produced a little plastic cup full of ice chips, and Jocelyn was amazed at how wonderful the ice made her throat feel. The ice made everything better.

She was luxuriating in the absolute silence of her own mind, enjoying the icy sensation with full-blown appreciation, when "Jocelyn, we can keep you safe" broke the spell, and all the beeping and humming of the monitors roared back into her world.

"Safe from what? I didn't do anything." Then she remembered that maybe she had. The floppy disc with the emails. She had to think this through, but she knew she wasn't in any sort of mental state to deal with anything. She chomped another piece of ice. "You know what? Maybe you should go. I want to eat my ice."

The nurse smiled at Jocelyn and glared at Witherall. "She'll see you in a few days, Mr. Witherall. She's not going anywhere."

Witherall sighed and nodded, first at the nurse and then at Jocelyn. He collected his paper with the funny marks on it. Without looking at her, he folded it in half and then in half again.

"What does that say?" Jocelyn asked. "Does anyone know?"

He made eye contact with her and gave a hint of a smile. "Oh, yes. It was pretty easy to figure out. It's in English using 'Wingdings 3' font. It says: I am the ghost in the machine, and I love you."

CHAPTER FIFTY-TWO

IT WAS SOMETIME in the middle of the night. They had removed the drainage tubes hours ago, and now she was in a new place—a private step-down-unit room. There weren't nurses everywhere anymore, but all the beeping and sounds of technology steadily pulsed on. Jocelyn had begun to appreciate the song of her life as it played on stronger and stronger. She realized that as she lived, her online alter ego that she had been so attached to, LadyLiberty70, was dead. The hologram of liberty that she had been worshiping had been effectively shattered. She thought about that for a while, and she really wasn't sad; actually, she was kind of angry. Mostly, she was just sort of amazed that she was even aware of it. She took a deep breath (as deep as she could) and smiled because now she really was alive. The morphine was nice, too.

As she waffled between sleep and boredom, she reminisced about how sweet Jerry was. Jocelyn really hoped that he would get to be the ghost he always wanted to be. She snuggled under her hospital blankets and closed her eyes, contentedly thinking about all the sleepers who would be waking soon. That's when she heard the door to her room open. She kept her eyes closed. She didn't want to deal with the night nurse. She only opened them when she realized that her bed was moving. There were two men dressed in white unplugging her from the machines.

"What's going on?" she asked.

"Oh, we're transferring you. Just relax," the first man quietly said as he wheeled the stretcher up next to her bed.

"You'll be there soon," the other man whispered close to her ear as the two of them heaved her up and over onto the stretcher. He had minty breath. The other man grabbed her IV stand and gathered up all the seemingly extraneous tubes and wires. The Minty Whisperer strapped her arms down as the room fell eerily silent, devoid of mechanical reminders of her vitality. He pushed the stretcher, and she felt the inaudible rhythm of the plastic wheels rolling over the linoleum. Meanwhile, the guy holding the IV stand went over to the door and seemed to be making too much of a big deal about looking both ways down the hallway.

"Wait. Where are we going?" Jocelyn asked the man pushing her.

"Not far. But you need to be quiet. People are sleeping."

The man at the door made some sort of hand signal and whipped open the door. Jocelyn's stretcher flew down the hall faster than she would have ever thought possible. The man rolling the IV stand was now running ahead of them.

Worried that she was being rushed to the operating room, Jocelyn panicked and shouted, "What's going on?!" The man running up ahead looked back, made another hand gesture and that's when a terry cloth washcloth got jammed into her mouth. Jocelyn's eyes sprung open wide with fear. She struggled to free her arms from the restraints and tried to spit and push the washcloth out of her mouth with her tongue, but it wasn't working. Bound to the stretcher and weakly thrashing around, she watched the hospital signage flying by. Jocelyn noticed that it looked like they were headed to the emergency room. They blew past random nurses, late-night drunks and disorderly ER patients, and headed straight to the ambulance dock. The guy with the IV stand got there first and threw open the doors. The second guy kicked something under her stretcher and it lurched wickedly as it collapsed to the level of the awaiting emergency vehicle. The two men hoisted her, still strapped to the stretcher, into the ambulance. They both hopped in, too, and as soon as the doors were slammed shut, the siren started blaring. The ambulance tore out onto the highway on ramp.

"Oh man, guys. What are you trying to do? Choke her to death?" admonished a familiar voice from the front seat. The washcloth was removed from her mouth by one of the guys in white as he headed to the front passenger seat. She glared at the man and painfully tried to twist around to see who had said that, but she was still strapped down and her body hurt. "Joss, are you okay?" the voice asked.

Jocelyn's heart stopped. Her breathing stopped. Everything stopped. "Ethan?" she called over her shoulder.

"I'm getting you out of here, Joss. Don't worry. You're safe."

Jocelyn squeezed her eyes tightly and opened them, hoping that she'd somehow stop hallucinating. Alas, it wasn't an hallucination. She couldn't stop anything and was still bopping around in an ambulance. The guy in white was adjusting the tube to her morphine now. More pissed off than confused, she shook her head at the man and sputtered, "You... you! Why are you doing this?" The man, whom Jocelyn was just noticing had long dark hair pulled back into a ponytail and a full sleeve of tribal looking tattoos, didn't answer or make eye contact. He just kept fiddling with her IV. Then turning her attention back to the two guys in the front seat, she yelled, "Ethan! What the hell?!" It hurt so bad to yell like that. She wished she had some ice as she swallowed hard and winced.

"We're taking it all down, Joss," Ethan shouted back over the siren as they rumbled off toward the airport. "It's time."

"Time for what?"

"Time to clean house. Time to wash it all away and start over."

"Ethan, I don't know if you've noticed or not, but I'm half-dead! I have no idea what you have in mind, but this is messed up! Stop what you're doing! Stop!"

"Sorry, Joss. It's on. Kill or be killed time." That was the last thing she heard while resisting a drug-addled sleep.

“Those who make peaceful revolution impossible will make violent revolution inevitable.”

-John F. Kennedy

END OF BOOK THREE

LOOK OUT FOR BOOK FOUR:
THE PEANUT BUTTER PIPELINE
COMING 2016

NOTE FROM THE AUTHOR

MANY OF THE TOPICS IN THIS BOOK, as well as this trilogy you have just read, are based on real life events. I got the inspiration for the character of Jocelyn McLaren when I was elected to attend the 2012 Republican National Convention. Being disillusioned by the entire political process, I unaffiliated from the party as soon as I got home.

I'd like to thank Catherine Austin Fitts for her insight into the topic of Shadow Banking and Dark Money as well as all of the people in my life who have inspired this story. Unknowingly, their influence has shaped characters whom I love and are now a part of me. I genuinely hope that you have enjoyed inviting these characters into your life as well.

To see my real time tweets from the 2012 RNC, where I did dress as Jocelyn and pass out business cards just like the ones in this book, please visit Twitter **@JocelynMcLaren**. You are, of course, invited to visit **www.rachaellmcintosh.com** to stay up to date with my writing and appearances.

See you there!

www.ingramcontent.com/pod-product-compliance
Lightning Source LLC
Chambersburg PA
CBHW070834020826
48982CB00019B/1156/J
9780692504451